PACESETTER

THE SCHEMERS

HELEN OVBIAGELE

CONTENTS

DEDICATION

*I dedicate this book to the memory of my late grandmother, **Mrs Rebecca Onaiwu Edoh-Osunde**, who talked to me so much about life.*

CHAPTER 1

Cynthia stepped out of the scented bath in her luxurious bathroom, towelled herself, and stood in front of the full-length mirror to examine herself critically.

'Cyn, darling,' she cooed at herself, 'I give you pass marks. You still look good. That body doesn't look like that of a forty-nine-year-old recently retired nurse who has put thirty years into a profession which saps you physically and emotionally. You look quite ready to start another phase in an interesting life, this time involving slowing down and deliberate idleness. You've worked very hard all your life and you haven't done badly. After twenty-eight years of marriage, with two children who've left home, you're still very much cherished by **Uzo**, your husband, a prominent lawyer and traditional chief. Soon, he might be elected a Senator and, from there, he's sure to rise to higher positions. Your daughter, a pharmacist, is married with a child. Your son, a budding architect, is doing passably well at his studies. Your health is good. You have two houses in Britain, one back home in the Caribbean in **St Lucia**, this one here in **Enugu**, and a country house in **Eziuta**, your husband's village. Tell me, what problems do you have? None. Isn't life going to be a ball from now on? It is. So, go on. Enjoy yourself.'

Cynthia smiled, did a waltzing turn, and then went into the bedroom to get dressed. She sighed with contentment as she stood in front of her wardrobe trying to decide what outfit to wear. Since she was not going to go out, should she not remain in her housecoat all day and change into something smart just before her husband was due back in the evening? No, someone might turn up. Instead she chose an **adire** trouser suit, applied light make-up, and declared herself fit to receive anyone.

She was heading for the kitchen to have her usual breakfast of a glass of orange juice when the doorbell went. Who could that be? She looked at the kitchen clock — it showed ten minutes past one.

Cynthia smiled smugly as she thought of all those poor people out there rushing about trying to earn a living. What a relief it was that she was no longer one of them. Here she was, feeling so relaxed and free that she was having her breakfast at lunchtime. There was no pressure, no tension.

Of course there were chores crying out to be undertaken in the house. The garden could be improved. Old **Goddy** the gardener hardly did anything except moan incessantly about the high cost of living and his bodily aches and pains. Cynthia had **green fingers** and she enjoyed gardening, but since she had retired, she had decided to give herself a break there as well. The curtains needed changing, but at the moment she had no desire to engage in all the hassle of choosing the material and sewing it up.

She was rinsing out her glass when the doorbell went again. She paused, hoping that **Innocent**, their all-purpose domestic help of more than six years, had thoroughly vetted the caller at the gate before ringing through to the house. Cases of break-ins, forced entries, and armed robbery had become common in the **New Uwani Layout**, a place originally meant for the rich and/or the famous, but which was being shared by the lower middle classes, thanks to the zeal of a state governor who wanted to break down the social barriers between the rich and the poor. A housing estate containing blocks of flats for working-class people had been built directly behind the Layout, with only a high wall topped with barbed wire as a line of demarcation. Cynthia's street had the inconvenience of having its gardens overlooked by the blocks of flats. She and her neighbours loathed the situation but they could not leave the dream houses in which they had planned to spend the rest of their lives, so they had to put up with uninvited spectators when they used their tennis courts, swimming pools, or entertained in their gardens. Those who could raised their already high fences, but this did not totally solve the problem.

'Who's at the gate, Innocent?' Cynthia said into the intercom in the kitchen.

'Madam, it's a woman. She says she wants to see you.'

'What about?'

'Er, Madam, she says it's personal and that she won't take up much of your time. Her name is **Miss Chinwe Dozie**.'

'I see. Well, if you're sure she's not a robber...'

'I don't think she is, Madam,' said Innocent with a chuckle. 'She lives in the neighbourhood on the other side.'

'All right, lock the gate and bring her in.'

'Yes, Madam.'

Cynthia went into the sitting room to await her visitor. It could be someone who needed some medical advice, she thought. From time to time, women from the housing estate called on her with one health problem or another. Even though she had never found this very convenient, she never sent any of them away. She did her best to help.

'Come in,' she called to a soft knock on the door. Innocent ushered in a slim, dark-complexioned woman of about thirty, and then withdrew.

'Good morning, Madam,' Cynthia greeted her courteously. 'Please sit down. What can I do for you?'

The woman returned her greeting with indifference and sat down. Everything about her was just about average — looks, height, dress, and make-up. She swept Cynthia and the entire room with a cold, haughty look and crossed her legs.

'What can I do for you?' Cynthia asked again, trying to control the impatience that was rising in her.

'I'm **Chinwe Dozie (Ms)**,' said the lady slowly, fixing her hostess with an arrogant stare. 'I live in one of the flats over there, but I should be living in this house.'

'You should be living in this house?' asked an amazed Cynthia. She looked at the other with more interest. Was she in her right mind? 'Why?'

'Because I'm expecting a baby for your husband,' said Chinwe slowly and with a smile of satisfaction on her face.

If she had expected the other woman to fall down senseless or jump up to shout hysterically and attack her, she was greatly disappointed.

Cynthia uttered a short laugh and cleared her throat. She was dead calm both on the inside and on the outside.

'You're expecting a baby for my husband? Well, I must congratulate you. Have you told him about it or am I the first to know?'

'You can't be the first to know. He told me when we met about eight months ago that he would like a baby with me, and every month since then we have been expecting pregnancy to happen.'

'And now it has. Congratulations once again. How did my husband take the news?'
'He was naturally very delighted and he

went to see my parents at once.'

'Is that so? How old is this pregnancy?'

'Oh, it's in its fourth month,' said Chinwe, smiling and patting her stomach.

That would be about it, Cynthia thought. Her expert eye had noted the lady's pregnant state, even in the loose print dress she had on, as soon as she had walked in.

'Why did you decide to come and tell me?' Cynthia asked with feigned anger. Actually the news had left her feeling totally unmoved and unthreatened, but she was not going to allow the silly lady to get away easily. She would frighten her a bit. After all, she had deliberately brought trouble into her house by coming to announce her condition.

'Well, your husband, I mean Uzo, er, I mean the Chief, kept dragging his feet about telling you about us, so I thought I should come and do so myself. The earlier you know, the better for all concerned. I don't want to be his bit on the side and I can never accept being a secret wife.'

'You've got a lot of nerve, Madam,' said Cynthia, getting up and advancing towards her. 'You took a great risk coming here, you know. I could dash into the kitchen, get a knife, and stab you. I could beat you and your baby to a pulp. You could disappear totally from the face of the earth.'

'Yes, you could do all that, but you would get yourself into trouble. I took the precaution of telling the Chief and my people that I would be calling on you today. In fact, if you go into your garden you will notice two men on the top balcony to the left across the fence. They are my brothers. We live almost directly behind you. Your hands are tied, Madam,' finished Chinwe, looking triumphant.

Cynthia uttered a strange laugh as she stood over the other, a faraway look in her eyes.

In spite of her brave front, Chinwe began to cower in her chair. Cynthia was a much bigger woman and looked very strong. She tried to get up but Cynthia pinned her down by the shoulders.

'My dear, you certainly took a great risk coming here with your news and delivering it with such arrogance and confidence. I could snuff the life out of you by placing my hands on your throat like this. All the rooms in this house are sound-proofed and your screams would not be heard anywhere. You may have taken all those precautions, but they don't assure your safety. How do you know that I would not want to get into trouble? My major desire might be to get rid of you and your baby. The outcome might be insignificant to me, whatever it was. The joy of seeing you die would be enormous in that case. I could do whatever I liked to myself afterwards. I'm not afraid to die.'

Chinwe began to tremble violently. The woman looked quite mad and quite capable of carrying out her words. She tried to speak but no words came out. She was still pinned down in the chair.

'Yes, I could kill you and cover you up,' continued Cynthia in a low, dreamy voice. 'When my husband comes home, I could kill him too. My children are grown up and they live in Britain, which is a second country to them. They won't suffer. I'll have something to leave behind if I decide to quit the world suddenly, but you won't have anything; you're just starting out. But why should I deprive myself of the joy of living? I'll escape from this country and live out the rest of my days elsewhere. How about that?'

She applied a little more pressure to the other's shoulders and then suddenly let go. Chinwe fainted from the unexpected release. When she came to, Cynthia coldly pointed to the door.

Chinwe struggled to her feet and staggered out of the house and towards the gate where Innocent let her out.

'Chinwe, you look terribly ill. What's the matter?' asked her mother solicitously when she got home. 'Where have you been?'

'I'll tell you later,' Chinwe answered brusquely as she made for her room. 'Stop fussing over me—I'm not a child.'

Chinwe's mother sighed. She was not offended by her third child's rudeness—she was used to it.

CHAPTER 2

Chinwe was not the most brilliant in the Dozie family, but she was certainly the most ambitious. Right from her early teens she had wanted a good life for herself. The flames of this desire had been fanned by the family's numerous stays in various parts of the country as her father, a railwayman, was transferred from one post to the other. Theirs was a lower middle-class family and living in railway quarters had given the children the opportunity to mix with others from a higher social level at school, in church, and at the various children's parties. **Mr and Mrs Dozie** were satisfied with their lot in life: their brood of six children, the slow promotions at work, and their social life.

Mrs Dozie engaged in petty trading to supplement her husband's income. They were not rich but they did not consider themselves poor, even though it was hard to meet all the bills on a regular basis. After a hard day's work, Mr Dozie liked a bottle of beer and a game of draughts with the other men in the neighbourhood. His wife tended the vegetable garden with the kids in the evening and at weekends, or went over to, or received, a neighbour and got engaged in a delightful round of gossip. On Sunday, there was the village meeting which was almost an all-day social event.

The children had all attended secondary schools and three had gone on to take a university degree.

Ironically, the three who had not gone to university were the ones who were able to get jobs. Two sisters were married and worked as secretaries in **Port Harcourt** and **Aba**. One brother worked as a graphic artist in **Lagos**. Chinwe, who had done Education quite recently, after a failed marriage, and the two boys, who were Science graduates, had been unable to find jobs in their respective fields.

Eager to earn a livelihood, the boys held

classes for **GCE** and **JAMB** examinations candidates somewhere in town, and they seemed quite content. Chinwe had been offered a teaching appointment in a private primary school, but she had not taken it. It was not the life for her. She did not mind children but teaching at any level was not her scene.

Apart from the poor remuneration and the regular late payment of salaries, it was not a high-powered job. She wanted a job where she could get on with or without hard work, something in a multinational company, she thought.

She was reasonably bright academically and was confident that she could handle anything. She had the dogged determination to pursue and get whatever she set her mind on. She had studied Education at the university because it had been the only course offered to her.

Chinwe loved her family but she loathed the way they accepted their lifestyle without a murmur. How could anyone be content with living just above the breadline in a low-income housing estate, with an old battered car which was more off the road than on it as the only family luxury?

She did not share their philosophy of '**what will be, will be**' and '**my good will always get to me**'. In her view, people with such an outlook on life lacked drive and guts and were bound to remain poor and unachieving all their lives. You have to make things happen for you. This was why after her secondary school education she had, against all advice, got married at the age of seventeen to a young and rich Hausa graduate from **Kano**, while her family was in **Zaria**. It had not been a totally loveless match, but the main attraction on her side had been the man's wealthy lifestyle. **Danladi** was not high up in the advertising company where he worked as a media executive, but his salary was supplemented by his wealthy businessman father. Chinwe, who was totally dependent financially on him, loved living it up, mixing with the rich and famous, and jetting from Zaria to **Kaduna**, to Kano, to **Jos** and even places as far flung as Lagos and Port Harcourt.

She acquired a taste for expensive things and she felt out of place whenever she visited her family in Enugu. It was always a relief to go back to Zaria and Danladi.

Her marriage began to disintegrate when her husband lost his job through retrenchment and they had to move in with his family in Kano. Chinwe and Danladi were given a chalet on the family estate where her parents-in-law as well as her brothers-in-law and their wives and children lived. She got on well with her parents-in-law but she somehow felt out of place. This was not because she was of the **Igbo** tribe while the others were **Hausa** and **Fulani**, but because she was the only wife or even female adult in the family who had no means of livelihood. Danladi's sisters-in-law and sisters were either workers, businesswomen, or students in higher institutions of learning. The days when the northern woman was raised strictly for a life in **purdah** were fast receding as she got as much education as possible and then went out to work. Chinwe felt a bit ashamed that, as one of the so-called progressive southerners, she had to become a 'kept woman'. She suddenly realised that her educational level was much too low to get her a job that was worthwhile in her eyes.

To add to her discomfort, her husband became sober all of a sudden, discarded high living (for which he had no more money anyway), and went all out to get a job. After a couple of months of intense searching, he got the job of a general manager with a motor company.

Chinwe heaved a sigh of relief as she expected the high living to resume, but it did not. She was disappointed and she sulked. Danladi had to have a stern talk with her.

'Look, Chinwe,' he told her, 'you're twenty now and I'm twenty-eight. We've been married three years and have no children. I think our major preoccupation now should be to start a family. We can't keep jetting around squandering money forever. We have to plan for the future.'

'Is it my fault that we have no kids yet?'

asked Chinwe indignantly. 'I've had several tests and doctors have told me that there's nothing wrong with me.'

'That's right, but they also said there's nothing wrong with me either,' countered Danladi pleasantly. 'I think we've not been very serious about starting a family. We've not really concentrated and observed the very simple rules doctors have said will help make it possible.'

'Well, you said we were too young to start having babies so soon. It was only when **Mama** started expressing some concern last year that we went to see the doctors,' said Chinwe sulkily.

'That's true. My mother did express some anxiety, and I did say initially that we should not saddle ourselves with babies right away. We are older now and I think we would make very sensible parents. Look at my brothers and their wives—they make such a complete family with their kids. Sometimes I'm envious of them. Their wives are so industrious and achieve so much, just like my mother.'

'I can be achieving and industrious too,' said Chinwe with some asperity.

'I'm sure you can. I'm not complaining about finance. After all, I didn't marry you so that you could slave away at work to help supplement the family income. I can look after you. Just concentrate on looking after me and the house; then make babies for me. Not lots—just five or six.'

He kissed her, and they both laughed, but Chinwe's discontent began that day. The happy-go-lucky life she had cherished seemed gone forever.

Danladi returned home each evening too worn out for a cosy chat and their usual hectic and enjoyable love-making. It became something reserved for the weekend only, then it became fortnightly, and finally just once a month. Joy went out of it and it became merely a routine.

Chinwe would not have minded if there had been parties to look forward to. She was usually alone in their chalet all day. Every morning she would look with envy through the window as her sisters-in-law were whisked off to work in their personal or official cars. Then her mother-in-law would be taken to her shop.

Chinwe began to develop an **inferiority complex**. Of all the wives in the family she was the youngest, the least educated, and the only one without children. She had a lot of time to brood and she knew that the other wives looked down on her. The condition would have been bearable if the high-living, high-spending life had still been there. She regretted not heeding her family's advice that she should have obtained a higher qualification and got a job before getting married. If her man refused to give her a good life at any stage of her life she would be able to do so herself.

She began to lose interest in her home and soon Ladi got fed up with her dark moods. He began to spend more time with his extended family; sometimes he would return home and say he had already had dinner. Chinwe was too full of resentment and self-pity to even notice the warning signs of a marriage which was falling apart, or perhaps she did not care. She felt she deserved a better life than the one she was living. Ladi began to ignore her.

One day he told her that, since they were both unhappy with each other and there did not seem to be any hope that things would improve, he felt it was best for them to be apart for six months so that they could sort out their feelings. He told her that, though as a Muslim he could take on more wives, he believed in monogamy. He said he was still fond of her but it appeared her heart was no longer in the marriage. To his disappointment she did not put up any defence or tell him that she still loved him. She simply agreed to the separation and said she would go to her people in Enugu. Actually, she had never intended to remain Ladi's wife for life. Her plan had been to make useful connections in his social circle, have a terrific time, secretly amass some wealth, and then beat it back to her people. She had not wanted the complication of kids being shuttled between one parent and the other, so she had secretly gone on the **Pill** to avoid pregnancy. Her family was not happy that her marriage had ended so soon and abruptly, and without any children, but she was made to feel welcome all the same. Chinwe, however, hated everything around her: the flat in the housing estate her parents had retired to, the neighbours who she felt were of an inferior social class to hers, and the humble lifestyle of her own family.

She had enrolled for GCE classes and, with some help, she got admission to do Education in one of the new universities.

At the end of the agreed six months' separation, she had written to Ladi informing him of her intention to go on for further studies. He had supported the idea and, when she was offered admission, he sent her a large sum of money to cover the entire four-year course. A month after this, he came down to Enugu to announce to her family that he considered their marriage over. Her parents pleaded with him to give her a second chance but he told them that he did not think Chinwe would ever find total satisfaction in their marriage. Even if they gave the marriage another try, it would fall apart again because she would still be discontented. He did not actually know what Chinwe wanted out of life and it would be unfair of anyone to expect him to hang around her forever, waiting for her to find happiness and satisfaction with him. He had his own life to live.

Just as previously, Chinwe did not put up any defence. Inwardly, she was sad that Ladi did not want her any more, but she did not really regret the end of the marriage.

For the next four years she buckled down to work at her university up north. Towards the end of her course she met **Ifeanyi**, a good-looking postgraduate student from Aba. For the first time in her life, Chinwe was very much in love. Ifeanyi, who was about Ladi's age, was fond of her too but he had a steady girlfriend of several years' standing who was reading Law at the **University of Nigeria, Nsukka**. When Chinwe wanted something, she went all out to get it, so, within a few months Ifeanyi had broken off with his girl and become hers.

On graduation she persuaded him to go to Enugu, where he had some relations, to look for a job so that they could be together and get organised for the future. After some search he finally got a job in a **Public Relations** outfit. The salary was not much but it was a job full of glamour—lots of partying, mixing with important people, and travelling. In a short while he became a real **man-about-town** and Chinwe was very proud of him as she accompanied him everywhere.

In spite of his popularity he remained level-headed and worked hard at his job. They discussed marriage and they decided to save up for it. The snag was that Chinwe was unable to land any job—even in the teaching field. She refused to join the growing number of young people who gave lessons to pupils preparing for internal and external examinations. She wanted something more out of life, so she remained unemployed, and had to rely on those around her for money to spend.

This hurt her pride very much and she became almost impossible to live with. After two years of intense job-hunting, she became depressed and stopped even trying. With lots of time on her hands she began to take more notice of the residents on the posh side of the Layout. Life was so unfair. While residents of the low-income housing estate lived on the breadline or, at best, a little above it, their fellow human beings on the other side led a life of ease and opulence. Some of their graduate children might be unemployed too, but they were not depressed about the situation as no member of the extended family had been eagerly awaiting their graduation and subsequent landing of plump jobs so they could render financial help to relations. They zoomed around in their parents' cars, and the very wealthy ones went abroad to ease the boredom in between job-hunting.

Living so close to the line of demarcation on the housing estate, and being forced to observe the difference in lifestyles, was

sheer torture to **Chinwe**, even more so
when she had already savoured, some years
before, what it felt like to be extremely rich.
When she first went to live with her parents
after her graduation from the university,
she had been so taken up by her relationship
with **Ifeanyi** that she had hardly noticed
other people. It was during one of his trips
out of **Enugu** that she had had the time to
observe the neighbours. She had known
some of the rich ones vaguely through
discussions with her family but she had not
really met any of them. She became a
reluctant witness, however, to the part of
their private lives which was displayed in
their backyards, as her family lived on the
fourth floor of their block of flats.

CHAPTER 3

The **Ubanis** fascinated Chinwe the most. Their house was only average, compared with the fabulous houses on their street, and they were not all that over-wealthy, but they were certainly the most well-known pair. **Chief Ubani's** law firm was a popular one and he had defended many famous cases in the law courts. His **West Indian** wife was an experienced nurse who had appeared regularly on a television health programme. Many women on the housing estate, including Chinwe's mother, still took their health problems to her.

Chinwe had never met the Ubanis, even though they were familiar faces to her. She liked the husband, a short, greying man who carried himself proudly with a constant friendly smile on his face. He looked his best in tennis gear or swimming trunks—he had such nice legs. However, it was not his sex appeal which had heightened Chinwe's interest in him; it was the power and popularity he wielded. It was too late to wish for such a father. How she envied his children whom she had never met! She used to fantasise about the incredible sort of life she would have led as the daughter of such a man.

As her interest in him grew, she began to feel a dislike for his wife. How did she deserve such a man? She was nothing in looks or in education, and she could only produce two children! Fancy a wealthy and prominent **Igbo** chief having only two children! Come to think of it, why did he have only one wife? Men of his calibre, irrespective of having foreign wives or having contracted church or registry weddings, had at least two wives to enhance their prestige in society. Usually, after a while, the legal wife would no longer be constantly seen at the side of the prominent man as she gradually gave way to a much younger wife. It should be very easy to dislodge a foreign wife. One hint of trouble and she would scuttle back to wherever she had come from, to be heard of no more.

Dislike for **Mrs Ubani** soon turned into hatred. Why should a foreigner come and enjoy such a lifestyle? What hold did she have over the man? What about the man's people? Has she been accepted by them? The Igbo family tie was very strong and a wife had to merge in very well for her home to be a happy one. If your in-laws accepted you, you were all right for life, for they would rally round with their strong support whenever you had problems—particularly marital ones. If their son rejected you and the union broke up, they would continue to support you and your kids in whatever way they could.

'Oh, Mrs Ubani is well accepted by her in-laws,' Chinwe's mother told her. 'From what I have heard, they did not even insist that the husband take another wife so he could have more kids when he had told them that she could not have any more than the two she already had in Britain.'

'That's strange, very strange,' scoffed Chinwe. 'How can a man of his prominence have only two kids? He must have girlfriends who would only be too willing to have as many kids for him as he desires. I understand he has a roving eye and is quite fond of women.'

'Well, many men are that way; even those without any claim to money or fame,' said **Mrs Dozie** with a tinge of scorn.

Chinwe smiled. 'Mama, you're still upset about Dad's casual fling with **Mama Nnena** and a few other women some years ago.'

'Wouldn't you be? Eh? There I was, working my fingers to the bone so we could save up for a deposit on this flat, while he was busy warming these women's beds behind my back—and their husbands' too. Women who were much older than I! Hm!'

'Relax, Mum,' consoled Chinwe. 'Dad was naughty but he didn't really do any harm. He had just retired, he had a lot of time on his hands, and these women were available. So he...'

'Then, what about the money he spent on them, eh? Money we could not afford to fritter away.'

'I don't think Dad's ever had money to spend on women. Even if he had, he wouldn't. He's too sensible and thrifty for that.'

'Are you saying he got those women's favours for nothing? Grow up, Chinwe. Those women would never do such a foolish thing. Give their bodies for nothing! You must be joking. Your Dad must have paid heavily for their services—services he didn't need. Hm, I'm still so angry.'

'Cool down, Mum. Dad was most repentant when he was found out, and I'm sure he wouldn't do anything like that again.'

'Is that so? He only has to be financially comfortable for him to be tempted again.'

'Well, don't allow him to get financially comfortable. Take every **kobo** he has off him. That should be very easy — he's only a pensioner who is partly dependent on you and his children for most of his needs. You shouldn't feel threatened at all. No woman would be anxious to take him from you, however virile he still is. Besides, his health is poor. He would be a liability to them.'

'Ha, ha, ha!' laughed Mrs Dozie heartily. 'You're right, Chinwe.'

'I think I am, Mum,' said Chinwe, who was beginning to get bored by the conversation.

She soon switched back to her pet subject of the moment—the Ubanis.

'So, what hold has this woman over him that he wouldn't marry another wife or have kids outside the marriage?'

'You sound a bit bitter, Chinwe,' her mother said in surprise. 'What have you got against this woman?'

'I hate—no, not hate—I dislike a situation where a foreign woman enjoys such a stable and comfortable marriage with one of our men who normally treat their Nigerian wives shabbily.'

'There are many Nigerian men who are nice to their wives—even to those who are childless. Your father is nice to me.'

'He is, but then he has to be. You're

everything to him—mother, wife, lover, sister, and friend, and you work hard to keep the family happy. Any man would be nice to you.'

'Thank you, Chinwe. Maybe Mr Ubani is nice to his wife because she has helped him a lot in the past. Many of our men who studied abroad married those foreign women who had helped them financially. It was a way of compensating them. This woman must have done a lot for her husband and that may be the reason why he has not allowed his relations to interfere in their marriage. I like him. He's a man of integrity. They are so happy together. It's the lady's luck to land such a nice man. She's nice too. She's been of immense help to many of us here on the estate.'

Chinwe turned away in disgust. Her mother was too easy-going and complacent to agree that Mrs Ubani did not deserve such a man. She had no right to such happiness and stability in her marriage.

Chinwe decided in her heart there and then that she would take Mr Ubani from his wife.

She could not have him for a father; she would have him for a husband instead. She wanted a good life with a man who had already made it and who would feel too old and respectable to mess around with other women. Well, she wasn't too sure about the last bit, but with a new family, such a man would be so thrilled that he would behave well. Men are more patient and tolerant fathers and husbands with families they acquire in their old age, she thought.

Suddenly, the gloom which had settled on her for some time lifted, and her heart became lighter. She could see the pattern for the rest of her life clearly. She was going to have a nice and comfortable home with a man she admired. It was a pity it was not going to be with Ifeanyi, whom she loved very much, but she had come to the conclusion that it would be a very long time before he would be able to give her the sort of life she really liked and deserved. He might never be able to, for he had a lot of financial responsibilities in the extended family. Life with him would have been loving and tender, but the thought of a

possible poor lifestyle due to financial
obligations to her husband's people
frightened her.

Chinwe smiled as she began to make plans
for seducing Mr Ubani. It was a pity she
could not take her mother into her
confidence. They got on well but she would
be horrified to know that her daughter was
cold-heartedly plotting the ruin of a couple's
happy union. Her mother lacked drive and
ambition. All she believed in was endless
hard work and devotion to her family.

Chinwe did not want that sort of life for
herself. She was very aware that she was
not a raving beauty and that, short of
flinging herself at him, Chief Ubani would
never notice her, let alone approach her for
a romantic relationship. She also knew from
information gathered that he hardly ever
initiated a relationship with women; instead
he was chased after by women of all
categories for one purpose or the other. He
had no regular girlfriend and indulged
mainly in one-night stands. He kept his
affairs well away from his house, although

Chinwe suspected that the wife must be aware of them. From all indications, he was very fond of her and was extremely careful not to make her feel any emotional insecurity.

'Well, that's the sort of husband I want for myself,' Chinwe decided. 'I don't want to share him with his wife or any other woman. His wife must go. She's old and she's enjoyed enough time with the man. She should go and live in Britain where her children are.'

She decided on the **hero-worship** approach. Access to Chief Ubani was difficult so she had to bribe his driver to make an abrupt stop to check the car, whenever he saw her at an appointed place when taking him to or from work.

It was two and a half nerve-racking weeks before anything happened.

'Oga, I want to check my tyres,' the driver told Chief Ubani on their way to work that morning. 'The car is not moving smoothly, sir. Maybe it's a flat tyre.'

'All right, park and check, **Okon**,' said the Chief, who was going through some papers. 'Be quick—we are quite busy today.'

'Yes, sir,' said the driver, springing down and taking a slow walk around the car, looking at the tyres.

Within the twinkling of an eye, Chinwe was at Chief Ubani's side of the car.

'Good morning, sir,' she greeted, bubbling with excitement.

'Good morning,' responded the Chief genially. 'Do I know you? What can I do for you?'

'Sir, I've called at your office several times in an attempt to see you for some legal advice for an aunt of mine who was recently widowed, but each time I was told you were out or busy. I was on my way there again this morning and I just could not believe my luck when your car stopped. So, maybe I can book an appointment to come and see you. I'm sorry, Chief, to burst in on you like this, but I didn't want to miss the opportunity of contacting you. I hope you don't mind, sir. I promised my aunt I would see you on her behalf.'

'Er, I don't mind—at least not much. I'm in a hurry, you see, and I really can't stop listening to your aunt's problems.'

'I understand that pretty well, sir. Maybe you can give me an appointment for much later. Perhaps next month or so.'

'Isn't the problem a pressing one? Can your aunt wait that long?'

'It's about her late husband's property, sir. His people have taken everything in spite of the fact that she had nine children for him.'

"A common case, that one,' commented the Chief, looking at his wrist watch. 'I'll give you a note for one of the lawyers in my chambers. He'll handle the matter.'

'Thank you very much, sir,' said Chinwe effusively. 'It's just that, er, er, my aunt can't afford legal fees and I had told her that since we are neighbours you might be willing to give advice for free; we don't want to go to the law courts if we can avoid that.'

'I see. Are we neighbours?'

'Sort of, sir. My family lives in the block of flats which overlooks your garden. I've been living and studying up north until recently but Madam, your wife has been quite helpful to my mother.'

'I see. Okay, come and see me in my office on, er, Saturday at ten. Bring your aunt along. I think I can spare just an hour on that day.'

'All right, sir. Thank you very much, sir.'

Chinwe left to make plans for the meeting. She was not naive in any way about how best to capture and retain a man's interest. Having been through one marriage and several relationships, she knew all about good personal grooming, charming personality, and prowess in the bedroom. She also knew of 'help' from spiritual churches and medicine men, although she'd never had cause to resort to these. She hadn't much faith in the supernatural process; she preferred to rely on what she could do by herself.

'Anything is worth trying if you really want
to capture a man,' counselled her childhood
friend, **Nwankego**. 'In this case, the man is
much sought after, so all avenues must be
explored. Potions and charms from the
native medicine people can be quite
effective, but I don't think they last as long
as the powerful prayers, oils, and perfumes
from the spiritualists in churches.
Moreover, as a believer, the latter is more
suited to your conscience.'

Nwankego was a personal assistant in one
of the state ministries and was regarded by
most people as a promiscuous woman. She
was a little older than Chinwe and she had a
kid each for four men and had never been
married.

'She's too conscious of her beauty to make a
good wife,' Chinwe's mother had predicted
during the girl's teenage years. 'She attracts
so many men that any man married to her
would go crazy with jealousy. I only hope
she can be a good mother.'

Nwankego was a good mixer and well liked
in social circles. She never lacked 'good

catches' but no relationship led to matrimony.

Chinwe did not regard her as a close friend, but she had to confide in her because she had this air of worldly wisdom about her.

So, before the meeting with the Chief, Chinwe found herself closeted with a **spiritualist** for many hours in prayers for 'love'. She was given 'blessed' olive oil, perfume, and soap to use in order to make Chief Ubani fall in love with her. It appeared these things worked, for after the first meeting at which no aunt had been present because she had taken ill suddenly, he told her he would like to handle the case personally. At the next meeting two weeks later she told him that, when her aunt's in-laws heard that she had contacted a prominent lawyer, they had become more cooperative and had promised that the aunt and her children would be given some of the property of their late brother.

'So the matter is closed, sir,' said Chinwe, getting up to leave. 'I knew that the mere mention of a famous person like you was bound to frighten them. Thank you very much, sir, for giving me some of your valuable time. I'll leave now, sir.'

'I'm glad the matter has been resolved amicably,' said the Chief, getting up from his chair. 'When will I see you again, Miss Dozie?'

'Call me Chinwe, sir. Do you want to see me again?'

'Of course. I like you, you know. You're so polite and respectful. What do you do?'

Chinwe told him all about her job hunting difficulties.

'I could give you some administrative duties here,' offered the Chief.

'I'll think about it, sir,' she answered. 'Thank you, sir, for the thoughtful offer.'

Working for him was not part of Chinwe's plans at all. In fact, she loathed the very idea.

At their next meeting there was no mention of it; apparently the Chief had decided it was not a good idea. Without any preamble they made love in a room adjacent to his office which he jocularly called his 'rest room'. Soon afterwards, he told her to drop the 'sir' and they were on a first-name basis. He was excited when she told him how much she admired his looks and his work. He had had such comments innumerable times from women, but it always boosted his ego when it came from a much younger woman. Chinwe's seeming **obsequiousness** and her hero-worship of him made him feel like a king. Instead of his usual one-night stand with women, he began to see Chinwe every Saturday. He made sure their affair was well-hidden and controlled. No telephone calls, no notes, or impromptu contact of any sort. They met in his office on a day appointed by him. Chinwe loathed all the secrecy, but accepted it because she felt it was only temporary. She continued seeing the spiritualist on a daily basis for 'fortification'.

Meanwhile she and Ifeanyi began to drift apart, to the chagrin of both. He wanted to know what was happening when she reduced the number of times she went out with him or called at his place.

'There's nothing wrong,' she lied. 'I feel I shouldn't monopolise your time so much and disturb your work. Tagging after you all the time won't do. I get jealous when all those ladies fling themselves at you at your official functions. For my sanity, I should give you breathing space.'

Ifeanyi accepted the explanation. In a way, it was a relief to him, for even though he thought he would like to marry her, her continued state of unemployment would have to postpone marriage indefinitely. At thirty-four, he ought to settle down in the next year or two. His salary was bearable, but he could not afford to have a wife who had no job. Chinwe did not seem to be making much of an effort to do any sort of work.

Ifeanyi began to regret breaking up with **Edna**, his former girlfriend. 'I feel so guilty about the break,' he confided in a friend. 'We were together for more than six years and were heading for marriage. She was so heartbroken.'

'Why don't you contact her again?' asked the friend. 'It appears you're still keen on her. Or are you simply feeling sorry for her?'

'I'm confused. Chinwe virtually swept me off my feet, but the effect is wearing off now and I wouldn't mind being back with Edna. She's doing her **youth service** with a newspaper in Lagos. I understand she's been promised a job in a publishing company here in Enugu later.'

'What about Chinwe?'

'Well, what about Chinwe? I love her but she seems a bit too much for me. She has her eyes on great heights and I don't know how she would fit into my family even though we are both from humble backgrounds.'

'Think carefully and make up your mind,' advised his friend.

Ifeanyi began to think of going back to Edna whom he gathered had no steady boyfriend yet. He loved her far less than he loved Chinwe, but she came from a fairly well-to-do family and her income, if they got married, would help a lot in finding the funds to cater for his extended family.

This seemed calculating but Ifeanyi felt it would be foolish not to face reality and contract a marriage which would ensure financial ease.

So, through friends and relations, and after much pleading with her, he got his relationship with Edna back on the road again.

CHAPTER 4

Chinwe went limp with relief when the doctor confirmed that she was expecting a baby. For the past eight months she had been desperate for pregnancy to happen. She was not all that fond of babies and she had not given a thought to what sort of mother she would make, but she had this notion that only a baby would make Mr Ubani firmly hers.

He would be proud to be a father again after more than twenty years' break. Whatever their age, men like to be known as **virile** and **fertile** and, from the little she knew about his home, it appeared that he had only two kids because his wife could not have any more.

Chinwe did not lose any sleep over his wife. She was going to be forced to leave in no time when he told her about the pregnancy, since most foreign wives took the issue of fidelity in marriage rather seriously. The Nigerian wife would stay put no matter the number of 'outside' wives and children, if the man had money and fame. Of course it was all 'because of the kids' and 'not wanting one's labour in the home to go unreaped' that she had to endure the humiliation of being tossed carelessly aside and forgotten there like an old and useless item.

If Chinwe had had her way, she would have rushed over to Mr Ubani with her news. Already she could see herself as the mistress in that fabulous house, and she dreamed of the changes she would make. However, she knew that she had to wait until the day she was due to see Chief Ubani himself because he was a **stickler for routine** and he hated stubbornness and disobedience.

Her parents were speechless with fright when she told them she was expecting a baby for their rich neighbour. They had no idea she had been having a relationship with him alongside Ifeanyi.

'This is dreadful,' moaned her father with

his head in his hands. 'How can you have a romantic relationship with a married neighbour, let alone get pregnant for him? His wife has been of immense help to your mother. How can we ever raise our heads again in this area when the news breaks out?'

'Oh, my God!' exclaimed her mother. 'What you've done is callous. You have your own boyfriend and you go running after a married man old enough to be your father! That's a sin. What's wrong with Ifeanyi? I know you love the good things of life and he is not rich, but he comes from a good family and has a lot of prospects.'

Leave Ifeanyi out of this, Mother,' said Chinwe, getting annoyed.

'Well, he's the man you introduced to us as someone you're likely to marry,' said her father. "We would like to have grandchildren through you and we were most unhappy when your marriage ended without any issue. But if you have a nice boy like Ifeanyi who is fond of you and who is willing to marry you, why have a relationship with another man? Allowing yourself to become pregnant for a married man was most foolish. Ifeanyi would drop you at once if he got to know. Mr Ubani is happily married—he can't marry you. If he wanted extra wives and kids he would have acquired them by now. He's a very powerful man in this state and he's gunning for a political post at the next elections, so he will not want to be involved in anything which might tarnish his image.'

'How will a baby or wife tarnish his image?' asked Chinwe. 'This is Africa—extra wives are accepted in any form of marriage here. I don't see why his political ambition should be adversely affected by his home. Our rulers' homes have never been up for scrutiny. No one here resigns from a position because of his extra-marital affairs. I can't understand all the fuss about this pregnancy.'

'Your comment may be true for society, Chinwe, but that does not make the situation right,' said **Dele**, her younger brother, who had been a silent listener all along.

'You'd better watch it, Dele,' cautioned Chinwe. 'You don't know what your attitude about women will be later in life, especially when you've made it financially. Anyway, I refuse to accept that I've done anything I should be ashamed of or have regrets about.'

'Is that so?' asked her father. 'Well, I know you're an adult who's had a childless marriage, but the only way out of this matter, which I consider a mess, is the termination of your pregnancy. I hope you've not told Mr Ubani about your condition?'

'Ah, ah, ah,' cried Mrs Dozie in anguish. 'I don't support an **abortion**. I don't support it at all. Chinwe could die in the process.'

'She could also die in the process of childbirth,' said the husband.

'Heaven forbid such a calamity. That will never happen to our children. A point to consider is that this could be the only child Chinwe is destined to have.'

'Why should that be?'

'Well, we don't know, so that's the reason why this pregnancy must not be terminated.'

'You're wrong, woman. I don't support abortion either, but if a baby is going to ruin a home and cause much unhappiness, its birth should be prevented, particularly at this early stage. Chinwe, didn't you say you've only just missed your period?'

'Yes, Papa, but I'm going to keep this pregnancy whatever anyone feels or says. I've told Mr Ubani and he's very thrilled,' lied Chinwe.

'I don't believe you,' said her father. 'How can he be? How will he explain you and the baby to his much-cherished wife? Don't deceive yourself, Chinwe. Even if he's thrilled now, he's going to abandon you later. The man cares very much about his public image, I'm told. Have you ever seen him with another woman?'

'No, I haven't, but that doesn't mean he is faithful to his wife. He's very keen on me.

He wants me for a wife.'

'He wants you for a wife!' exclaimed both
her parents.

Dele smiled scornfully and left the room
quietly.

'Oh yes, he does, very much,' lied Chinwe
easily. 'In fact, he asked me to have a baby
for him so we can have a cast-iron reason
for becoming man and wife.'

Her parents were too shocked to say
anything for a while.

'Well, if that's the case,' said her father at
last, 'we'll wait for him to contact us about
the matter. If what you've just said is true,
he'll do the right thing by you. He's mature,
and a chief too. He knows what to do. We'll
wait.'

Two months went by. Chief Ubani did not
call at the Dozies'. He knew nothing of
Chinwe's condition. She had not told him
yet.

She told him when the pregnancy was three
months old. She had waited that long

because she wanted to be in a position to plead that her health would be at risk if he should suggest an abortion.

There was no need to inform Ifeanyi of her condition. He did not come into her plans at all. Anyway, he had not seemed to mind the coolness in their relationship.

She broke the news of her pregnancy to Chief Ubani at a point she considered tender and right one Saturday. Designing and calculating she might have been in establishing their relationship, but it was an anxious moment for her. Would he consider the whole thing a disgrace and injurious to his home? Would he reject her and the baby?

If he was angry he did not show it. He merely raised a surprised eyebrow and looked at her thoughtfully.

'You're expecting a baby?' he asked calmly.

'Yes,' she answered in a small voice, trying to look demure.

'For me?' he asked with some amusement in

his voice and eyes.

'That hurts, Chief,' she said in an offended voice. 'For whom else would I be expecting a baby?'

He let the question drop. He did not apologise. She had not expected him to. Chiefs and local celebrities have to keep up a haughty image.

'What do you want to do about it?' he asked, cutting into her thoughts.

His words startled her. She had felt an inward relief that he had neither been angry nor suspicious about the matter, but asking her casually what she wanted to do did not show any affection. It was as if making a baby with her was insignificant to him. Well, she would have to swallow her pride.

'I would like to keep it, Chief,' she said in a humble voice. 'I had not expected this to happen and as such I had not paid much attention when I missed a period. The doctor was not sure either when I went to him so he told me to wait for a couple of weeks as it might be a health problem I had.

When he told me it was pregnancy, I was dumbfounded and downcast because my religion forbids abortion. The only option I have is to have the baby.'

Chinwe stopped and waited for Chief Ubani to say something—make a pledge that he would accept the baby and marry her, or accept just the baby.

He said nothing. He just sat calmly at the far end of the settee watching her. She felt frightened by his calmness and the eerie silence in the room. The telephone rang, making her heart jump.

He reached out to take the call.

'Oh hello, **Cyn**,' he said, a smile breaking out on his face. 'Back from the shops already? Got all you wanted? Good girl! Oh, they've arrived already? Okay, tell them I'll be right over. No, no, ask them to wait. I haven't got much to do here really; at least nothing that cannot wait till Monday. See you soon.'

Chinwe seethed inwardly with anger and jealousy at the unfeigned affection Chief Ubani displayed while speaking to his wife.

Well, all that would soon stop. She wanted him all to herself and to live in that big house with her. She was not going to be tucked away in a small corner, known only as the mother of his 'outside' child, by him only, or perhaps by a handful only of his close friends and relations.

A **divorce** from his wife would be best, but she would not insist on this. She would settle for being a recognised second wife, by customary laws.

Chief Ubani, who had been busy gathering up his things, smiled at her and nodded towards the door. She hesitated. She would have liked a definite stand by him on the issue at hand. She realised a bit belatedly that there had been no love-making that morning. Its absence made her feel a bit out of control. Having him make love to her had always given her a sense of power. Seeing him reduced to a whimpering child craving to be made comfortable made her feel very important in his life. She was quite sure she gave him more pleasure and satisfaction than his wife. All the men she had had had been highly impressed by her performance which she had deliberately practised and perfected over the years, knowing that it would always be a valuable asset since she was neither wealthy nor a raving beauty. She was not promiscuous but she knew what the art was all about.

Even Chief Ubani with all his experience once remarked that she was **'hot property'**. That, combined with the spiritualist's fervent prayers had made her succeed where other women had failed. That is, not dropped by the Chief after a month or two, as was his normal practice.

Her condition notwithstanding, she must remain at all costs a 'hot property'. She made a sign at Chief Ubani who was standing near the door of his 'rest' room, waiting for her to follow him out. As she expected, he grinned, dropped his bag and in an instant was on the couch with her, breathing furiously.

The telephone interrupted them. 'Let it ring,' he said in a voice laden with passion. The ringing continued for a while and then stopped.

Chinwe smiled to herself with satisfaction. There was no doubt that it must have been the wife ringing to find out why he was still in the office. If only the stupid old cow knew what was going to hit her shortly, she would pass out. Chinwe smiled to herself again. She debated whether to make Chief Ubani stay longer with her or allow him to go to his wife. She felt swollen with pride. She only had to make a sign to get him whimpering once again. She decided to let him go. It was probably more sensible.

Although the doctor had told her that love-making was all right at that stage she would have to watch it. The baby, being the major weapon for carrying her plans to fruition, had to be protected by all means.

'Er, Chief, I hope you're not angry with me?' she asked him coyly.

'What about, Chinwe?' he asked, his thoughts clearly miles away.

'About my condition.'

'Your condition? Oh, I see what you mean. We'll discuss that when next we meet—that is, on Saturday the 12th. Here, take this.'

He gave her the usual envelope of money.

'Thank you, Chief,' she said humbly as she left the room and he let her out of the side door she usually came in and left by.

For the first time since their relationship had begun, she felt some humiliation. He was quite generous in his monthly handouts which had made her financially comfortable, but being pre-packed and given out in such a businesslike way made their relationship look cheap. She had not minded this before, but now that she was carrying his baby, a little show of affection would have been welcome, a gesture from him that he no longer considered her mainly a bedmate.

Chinwe did not find pregnancy comfortable and she became easily depressed even though her mother was very sympathetic and helpful. She would not be comforted as her condition had become quite obvious and the Chief was yet to make his stand known even two months after getting the news.'

Each time she brought up the subject he

calmly told her they would discuss it the next time. Initially this had not bothered her much since he had not rejected the pregnancy, but she began to worry when he did not increase her allowance to include expenses for the baby.

How was she going to get baby things which had become so costly? Already the allowance barely kept her and met her increasing medical bills. There was also the spiritualist's monthly allowance to be paid. To cap it all, her parents kept asking when the Chief was coming to discuss his intention about her condition with them. Her excuses that he was kept very busy by his work and political activities began to wear thin.

She was an impatient person and it had taken a herculean effort to control her impulse to engage in a verbal war with him which would force him to speak his mind on the issue. Their continued love-making notwithstanding, she wanted to know how he felt. **Nwankego** told her to be patient.

'Don't quarrel with him or he might

abandon you altogether,' she advised. 'I'm speaking from personal experience. The father of my second child, who's now four, turned his back on me when I kept insisting that he met my people. "Why should I meet your people?" he had asked me. "We never discussed marriage, let alone having a baby, so how do your people come into our relationship? We were just two adults having fun until you decided to get pregnant. You did not ask my permission to do so." '

'My goodness!' exclaimed Chinwe. 'Would a lover say all that simply to avoid taking on added responsibility?'

'Oh yes, that and even more. He told me at our next meeting that, while not dismissing the possibility that the pregnancy might be for him, he wasn't going to accept it for the very reason that we had not discussed having babies in our relationship.'

'Was it because he was married?'

'He wasn't married and he still isn't. He's only a couple of years older than me and I thought I had met someone who was free to settle down with me. We were so much in love. I hadn't wanted to get involved again with another married man, see where it landed me. He told me I was on my own and I've neither seen nor heard from him since that day.'

'You mean he has never seen the child?'

Nwankego nodded and subsided into a sad silence. Chinwe did not probe further. She felt sorry for the friend she had always envied.

Nwankego, although from a poor background, had got involved with people in the corridors of power right from her teenage years and she had been sponsored abroad by a generous 'godfather'. On her return, getting a good job and worthwhile promotion had come easily. Someone had built a small bungalow for her on Chief Ubani's side of the housing estate. She had lots of well-heeled admirers, but none got to the point of making her his wife. Of her four kids, only the first one was accepted by the father.

'Such a thing must never happen to me,'
thought Chinwe. To her, babies were a way
of binding a man so that one could live off
him comfortably. A baby whose father
rejected it would only be a liability to her in
terms of finance and emotion. She wanted
no part of such a life and she made up her
mind to force things to a head.

At the next meeting with Chief Ubani, she
boldly asked him when he was going to see
her parents. He was shocked and
momentarily lost his much guarded calm
exterior. Chinwe had timed her question
well. No definite stand by him: no love-
making. He came to her; she turned away.
After a couple of minutes' futile chase round
the room he sat down with his head in his
hands, moaning.

'When are you going to see my parents?'
asked Chinwe softly as she stood in front of
him provocatively.

Chief Ubani raised his head, looked at her
greedily and grabbed her. She turned away.
When he tried again, she allowed him near
and then repeated her question.

'Oh, soon, soon, Chinwe,' he said, hugging her tightly.

Later, as he gave her the usual envelope, she told him she needed money for baby things. She named a figure. He paused, then went into the next room. He brought back more money for her. She felt drunk with power as she forced him to name a date for the meeting with her parents. He did.

'Keep your promise, Chief,' she told him half-threateningly, her feigned humility tossed aside forever. 'As someone who wants a seat in the senate, you should honour your word at all times, even in a situation like this. Don't fail to turn up.' She opened the door and left.

Chief Ubani sat thoughtfully at his desk for an hour doing nothing. At last he left for home.

He did not show up for the meeting with Chinwe's parents.

It was then that Chinwe decided to carry the battle to his house.

CHAPTER 5

Cynthia sat in deep thought after Chinwe had staggered out of the front door. Images of her life with her husband **Uzoamaka** unfolded in her mind's eye as if it were a replay of a recorded event.

She had met him one day when he came to babysit for **Tunde** and **Fatima**, a young Nigerian couple who were tenants in her parents' terraced house in **London**. He was a law student and she was just at the beginning of her nursing career. She had knocked on the couple's door to say her customary 'Hi' on her way back from work when out popped this solemn-looking young man. He seemed extremely glad to see her.

'Ah, what a god-send,' he exclaimed in obvious relief, opening the door and trying to lead her in. She held back and looked at him suspiciously.

'Where's Fatima?' she asked.

'Come in first and then I can answer that question later. There's an emergency here for you, whoever you may be.'

'What emergency?'

'Come in and find out. Don't panic, I'm sure you can handle it as a nurse and a lady. Come in.'

'Where's Fatima? I know Tunde is due back any moment now, but Fatima should be in with the baby.'

'Oh, it appears you know the household well. Fatima's gone to meet up with Tunde somewhere for a meal or something. The poor girl needed the break, being cooped up all day with their little horror. Anyway, I'm a friend of theirs and I've come to babysit for them.'

'I see. That's nice of you.'

'Come on in.'

'I won't. I don't know you.'

'All right, we'll put that right now,' he said, grinning at her. 'I'm **Uzoamaka Ubani**. Twenty-five, single, and a Nigerian law student—a struggling one who's lived in this country for six years. I live a few streets away from here in **Hornsey—Rathcoole Avenue**, actually. Now you know me. Come in.'

'Okay, I'll stop by briefly then. I'm Cynthia. I live here with my parents. Fatima and Tunde are good friends of mine. What's the emergency you spoke about? Is something wrong with the baby?'

'Well, she's not cried for the past one hour—a rare thing with her when I babysit here, so I think something must be wrong. Come and have a look. She's just lying in her cot with her eyes shut. She never does that for long when I'm around, no matter what I do, she always hollers.'

He led Cynthia to the baby's cot.

'So, is she still alive?' he asked anxiously.

'Very much so,' said Cynthia with a smile. 'She's sleeping. All's well.'

'Thank goodness for that. I usually have murderous thoughts when babies cry for no just cause. I thought my thoughts when she was howling about an hour ago must have killed her. I had fed her, brought up her wind, changed everything she had on, and she just went on, wah, wah, wah. I had to put her in her cot.'

'You've coped very well. I must be on my way now.'

That had been the beginning of their relationship. They went out together only occasionally. He had his girlfriends and she had **Barry** who had been her boyfriend from her school days.

They had not been that much in love. For her their dates were just to break the monotony of her relationship with Barry.

Soon, however, she became more and more fascinated with him and his lifestyle. He took life, particularly his studies, very seriously, so seriously that he did not care much about his own comforts.

Fatima told her that most Nigerian students

in foreign countries were like that. They made sure they got the **golden fleece** they had come in search of. **Uzo** confirmed this, saying that it would be disastrous to go back home a failure, and find that the classmates he had left behind were far more successful. Cynthia had a lot of respect for him for this attitude. All her life she had been surrounded by youths who did not care much about a successful future. All they wanted was enjoyment now: and that involved endless and indiscriminate partying, getting drunk and stoned, skipping classes or work. With the girls, early parenthood was the norm. Many of her age-mates were single mothers who lived on social security. She and **Linda**, her computer-programmer sister, were considered achievers.

Within nine months she and Uzo had become steady in their relationship. She really loved Barry and it was not easy to drop him, but what sort of future had he to offer her? Very much the same as her father had given her mother. Casual and irregular employment; bouts of drunkenness and beating up of wife and kids. In short, not much of a stable and peaceful life, with a sense of responsibility and commitment almost at zero point. Uzo was well-read; Barry could not be bothered to be, even though the opportunities were there. He was a casual labourer on a building site and he moved with the usual set. He was nice, kind, and thoughtful though, particularly when he decided to keep off the bottle, which he did from time to time, to please her.

'Life with Uzo either in Britain or Africa would offer more thrills and security,' she had told herself. Fatima encouraged her relationship with Uzo—not that Cynthia needed much persuasion to team up with him.

She simply adored looking after him and organising him. He was terribly helpless in looking after himself in his tiny bedsit. He skipped meals and was always looking gaunt and hungry. She moved in with him so she could do the job properly. After a year of this, they jointly bought a house in

Finsbury Park and, on the completion of his course, they got married.

It was a blissful period for them as they lived the sort of marital life she had dreamed of—life with a humorous and responsible man who needed her. She looked after their finances and he was only too glad to let her do this while he concentrated on his career and earning enough to keep them both.

She wanted lots of kids and he did too, but later, circumstances pegged the number at two and they had to be content with this.

The issue of more kids raised its head when they came to **Nigeria** and he had to take a firm stand with the extended family after several meetings. This firmness enabled Cynthia to survive the first few years when she faced much hostility from his people who felt she had too much hold over him and seemed to control his life. They could not understand why he had so much regard for a mere woman, and only a wife at that. It was only a mother who deserved such devotion and consideration. On several occasions when the situation had become almost unbearable for her, she had contemplated taking the kids and returning to live in Britain in their house there. She had to be patient and stay, for apart from Uzo's staunch support for her, she did not relish the idea of abandoning him. He would be helpless without her and she would miss looking after him.

They were so close that he told her to be calm and never to be afraid of being landed with mates or 'outside' kids for him by other women, openly or secretly. He told her that he owed it to her to give her emotional security. She had given up so much for him. To make her feel ever more secure and comfortable, they built or bought houses in both their names. However, the one in his village bore just his name while the others bore **Cynthia** and **Uzoamaka Ubani** or just her name. He explained to her that the contents of a will were hardly ever respected here by the extended family who normally move in to inherit a man's property when he died, and that many wives felt reluctant to take their in-laws to court when they were dispossessed of their husband's property for fear of their children being ostracised from the family.

Cynthia felt touched that Uzo was being so considerate, and she decided not to worry about his womanising.

She knew, of course, that he loved women and enjoyed being adored by women. The poor man went to such lengths to conceal his affairs. She knew all about his 'rest' room. The various drivers and domestic helps they had had over the years had, without any prompting from her, kept her abreast of the goings-on, because 'Madam is not of our people, and will never know of these things,' they had told her, to explain their seeming disloyalty to 'master'. She had listened in horror as they had told her that a man's mistress, through the use of powerful **juju** by a strong medicine man, could turn his head and he would send his wife and kids packing, and bring the mistress into his home.

Cynthia was not totally unaware of the existence of cult practices, for when she was young her mother used to complain that her paternal grandmother, who was living with the family then in London, practised **voodoo** and made her uncomfortable and ill with the smelly water she used to sprinkle on the staircase. Cynthia and her sister sympathised with their mother, but took the issue very lightly and did not really believe in the power of the occult. The fact that she had survived all the alarms about 'black magic', witches and wizards since she arrived in Nigeria was further proof that such things would not affect her.

'I live according to my conscience and I bear the consequences,' she had told **Funmi Ogbuagu**, a close friend and a colleague during all the years she worked at the state hospital.

'Fair enough, Cynthia, but you watch it,' Funmi had cautioned. 'It may be psychological, but unpleasant things do happen here when you have a woman who is desperate to eject you from your home.'

'God protects.'

'Yes, He does.'

'Your advice is sound, though. It's just that over the years I've built this shell of resilience which prevents problems from getting through to me. My husband admired me for this, but the fact is that I do get depressed by happenings inwardly. I have constant nostalgia for my childhood days back home and the British way of living.'

'That's normal. You've adjusted very well over here and you go on annual vacation to **St Lucia** and Britain. As soon as you retire you'll be able to do this more often. Lucky you. You have a good marriage and these days Uzo does not have many relations to look after financially, so you can afford to travel out. My husband and I are still heavily involved in the cumbersome task of training people in the extended family.'

'Yes, I should thank my stars,' said Cynthia. However, in her heart, there was an emptiness.

She would have loved to spend longer periods in St Lucia, lazing on the beach and tending the garden, with no care in the world.

Another attraction was the presence of Barry who, now a widower, had abandoned London life to live in St Lucia, and ran a restaurant with his only child. She was glad she had married Uzo, though sometimes she missed Barry's carefree attitude to life. He was always bubbling with energy no matter his circumstances. His small sense of responsibility compared with Uzo's serious disposition, which used to irritate her in those days, later became an attraction.

'Why care so much at work and at home?' she would ask herself when the going got tough. 'Cyn, you can't rid the whole world of misery.'

Her retirement was a big relief. She had slowed down her pace and she was going to live, live, live!

Things were going according to plan when Chinwe came with news of her pregnancy. The girl's audacity was amazing. Cynthia had felt really mad, but outward calmness was part of a nurse's training and she was well-practised in it.

The anger had lasted just a couple of hours. By the time Uzo returned home she was limp with emptiness. She was fed up with his womanising. He had been discreet, yes. But when would he stop? She felt disappointed that in spite of all his promises he had **his child**. Affairs could be ignored, but a baby could not be ignored. It was a serious matter, especially in their own case. He had limited her to having just two kids and at a time when she was past having children, he had allowed that sort of thing.

It seemed so unfair.

However, when she thought of the steps he had taken to ensure financial security for her and their kids, she felt comforted.

'Don't kid yourself, Cyn,' she told herself. 'Money and material things may not be everything, but they do help one cope with heartache in a situation like this. With the way things are, a comfortable old age beckons. I can settle anywhere.'

She decided there and then to be as cooperative as possible with Uzo, whatever his decision regarding Chinwe's pregnancy would be.

CHAPTER 6

Chief Ubani was terribly shaken when, as they were about to retire for the night, Cynthia told him about Chinwe's visit. He collapsed into the nearest chair.

'So, the thing is for real?' he said, half to himself. 'My goodness!'

He subsided into silence and his wife left him alone with his thoughts. He could not believe the dimension his relationship with Chinwe had taken. All along news of the pregnancy had seemed a dream to him which he was quite sure would vanish at any time. He had taken neither the girl nor her condition seriously. He knew all along that she was a desperate gold-digger and that she was not as humble and unassuming as she had earlier made out to be. Her threats later had not come as a surprise to him, but he had felt that all she had been after was to get more money out of him. He knew she looked pregnant, but he had not actually believed she was carrying a baby.

He had expected that, after getting a chunk of money from him to go and have the baby, she would disappear for a couple of weeks and then come back with the news that she had lost the baby. This had not happened to him before because he had been careful not to go beyond three or four months with any girl, but he had several friends who had had such an experience. It was a standing joke in his club. You inquired after a member's girlfriend and he would say, 'Oh, that one? She's left to have a **ghost baby**.'

Using pregnancy, real or fake, to get more money out of a **sugar-daddy** was accepted as part of the make-up of most young mistresses. Chief Ubani had made sure he was never caught in that web. Before a girl began to feel comfortable with him, he was off.

He could not explain how Chinwe had got him to keep her for close to a year. He had found her 'okay' as a lover, but she had not been the most fantastic. He knew he could be satisfied with just his wife if he made up his mind to be, but there was immense excitement in having secret affairs with a variety of women. Unfaithfulness had its thrills for him. He felt like a naughty schoolboy.

He had never dreamt that Chinwe was out to have a permanent relationship with him. This shocked him. He did not love her; he did not want her as a permanent fixture in his life. Why, in spite of their enjoyable love sessions, he hardly thought of her until his secret diary reminded him of their dates. How was he going to get himself out of the mess? He knew it was useless thinking of getting her to have an abortion. She had obviously made up her mind to have a baby for him whatever happened.

He joined his wife in the bedroom and gathered her up in his arms.

'I'm sorry, Cyn. I really am. Please forgive me,' he told her over and over again.

Cynthia quietly disengaged herself from him and made him sit down with her.

'I can't pretend that I've not been in hell since I got the news,' she said, 'but it's no use asking "Why?" and "How?" and all that. The thing now is, what are you going to do about it?'

Ubani told her all that had transpired between him and Chinwe.

'I can't understand myself,' he said in a bewildered tone. 'I seemed helpless whenever I was with her, and yet I care nothing for her. I thought she was out to get money, that's all. I didn't actually believe she was pregnant—not even when she kept urging me to go and see her parents. Look, Cyn, please forgive me. This was the last thing I would have wished for even if we didn't have such a good marriage. If only the tramp would consent to an abortion, I wouldn't mind paying whatever fee she asked for. I want nothing to do with her.'

'Well, I'm sure you don't, but she certainly wants a lasting relationship with you. You didn't promise her marriage or something?'

'Marriage? I said I didn't even acknowledge

the presence of a coming baby. I just allowed things to jog along. Oh, I've been a fool. How can I solve the problem? Anyway, that's a secondary issue. The main one is how to make you forgive me. I'm awfully sorry, Cyn. I really feel terrible. What will our children say? I can't give them this sort of emotional insecurity considering how close we all are. They don't deserve it. They have been good kids.'

He looked so distraught that Cynthia's heart softened and she held him close and told him that forgiveness was on the way, though she would require some time to get over the shock. He nodded miserably.

'Hm, you're lucky,' Funmi told her when Cynthia confided in her friend later. 'Many men here would tell you to go and do your worst if you insisted on a remorseful attitude from them. Some would apologise and then expect the relationship between you to go on as usual, with you making no fuss about the incident. Others would even tell you that they intend to bring the mistress in, particularly those who are chiefs and whom society normally expects should have more than one wife and a multitude of kids.'

'I know,' said Cynthia thoughtfully, 'but I don't expect that sort of attitude from Uzo, considering the fact that it was he who limited the number of kids we would have to just two.'

'Hm, how many men would acknowledge that later, or even remember it? Just thank God for giving you such a reasonable husband. You're extremely lucky.'

'I guess I am.'

'So what's the next step?'

'We want to see if we can get the girl to accept money and disappear from our lives. Uzo cannot reject the pregnancy at this stage because she has threatened to make their affair public and thereby ruin his political ambitions.'

'Oh, that won't work for her. His party will not reject him for having a mistress and an "outside" baby. That's his private life. We would have no male rulers if we scrutinised our men's marital lives.'

'I know. Wives and "outside" babies are accepted, but if she goes to the Press with the news that he has put her in the family way and then abandoned her, he might not get nominated for a senatorial seat. These days people are gradually becoming conscious of honour in the lives of public officers. She has proof that they have been lovers for close to one year.'

'Really? The scheming so-and-so!'

'I wonder what she really wants. Does she just want to have a baby for a "big" man so she will be comfortable for life?'

'I don't think that's it at all, Cynthia, dear. She wants to oust you and become the "madam" in this house.'

Cynthia was dumbfounded. 'Are you serious? I mean, she did say something like that, but I thought it was just to get me worked up enough to believe that she's really on with Uzo.'

'She meant every word of her intention.'

'But Uzo neither loves nor wants her. Have you seen the vixen? She's totally unsuited to be Uzo's wife—even a hidden one.'

'I'm sure she knows that. That's why she wants to make things very uncomfortable for both of you. She wants to be accepted, not as the mother of Uzo's child, but as a second wife. That's the first step. Later, she would see that she became the only wife. Sorry to paint such a horrible picture of the matter, but I'm sure you know that I'm not talking drivel.'

'I know you're not, Funmi,' said Cynthia with a sad sigh. 'Well, we'll see how things go.'

'Pray hard, Cynthia, pray hard. The girl's desperate. That sort never gives up. Oh, if only fate would smile on the issue and a miscarriage occur unprompted, then all would be well. I suppose that's a wicked thing to say, but why should someone deliberately want to use a baby to disrupt a happy home? Surely God will not allow that.'

'I suppose God knows best. After all, I might never have known of the matter if Uzo had cooperated with her and had gone to see her parents. He could have set her up somewhere secretly and even married her the traditional way.'

'Uzo would never do that to you. He would let you know.'

It was decided that Chinwe would be invited to Chief Ubani's office and told that all her hospital bills would be paid and that the child would be trained and looked after up to the age of twenty-one.

Cynthia did not think that Chinwe would accept the offer but she went along with her husband's suggestion.

Chinwe had arrived at the office thinking it was going to be the usual meeting with her lover. She was a little frightened when Cynthia casually walked into the 'rest' room. She got up to go, changed her mind and sat down.

Chief Ubani told Chinwe the decision he had made with his wife. She refused to speak for a while, looking at Cynthia with eyes full of hatred.

Cynthia stared calmly back.

The telephone rang in the adjoining room and the Chief got up to take the call.

'Madam, you feel triumphant, don't you?' asked Chinwe with a hiss and a short laugh. 'Be assured that I shall have the last laugh. You think you have him in the hollow of your hand? You don't. I do.'

'That's interesting,' observed Cynthia. 'What do you intend to do about this object in the hollow of your hand?'

'You'll find out,' said Chinwe with venom. 'You obviously can't satisfy him, Madam, and that's why he jumps from woman to woman. You're old and you leave him dead cold. He needs young blood to warm him up. He needs more kids too—kids you can no longer give him.'

'You're very bold, aren't you?' asked Cynthia in an amused voice. She had come prepared for the type of insults Chinwe would want to heap on her to upset her peace of mind and get her really mad.

'Let me tell you what you are,' she told Chinwe softly. 'You're a cheap whore from the filthiest gutter who thinks the only way to comfort is to snatch a man from his family. My husband only wanted to wipe his feet on you, like many men before him had, and will, but you decided to trap him with pregnancy. You're using threats to get him to accept the baby but that is not in your best interests. He can never love you or your child, no matter how much money he might decide to give you. You're ruining your own life. You should have had an abortion or accepted money to get you off the scene.'

'I don't want to get off the scene,' shouted Chinwe. 'I want the Chief and I'll get him in spite of you.'

'Hm, it depends on what you think you're getting,' said Cynthia in derision. 'I wish you good luck, anyway.'

"I should wish you good luck," said a demented Chinwe. 'You'll need it. I'm carrying the Chief's child and I intend to have it in his house. Now, a house with two women in it is a house on fire, so one of us will have to check out, and that person won't be me. You'll have to go; your time is up, and long overdue too. You have nothing else to offer the Chief. I do.'

'I see,' said Cynthia distantly. 'So how do you intend to eject me from my home? With blackmail about my husband's political ambitions?'

'That's my business,' snapped Chinwe.

Chief Ubani came into the room and Cynthia abandoned the scathing response she had for Chinwe and put on a sweet look.

'Cyn, dear, we'll have to leave soon,' said the husband. '**Innocent** rang to say that my parents are in town. I've just spoken to them. They're returning to the village this evening.'

'Let's go then,' said Cynthia, getting up.

'Yes, so where are we? What decision did you two arrive at?'

'I accept your decision, Chief,' said Chinwe meekly, getting up too. 'I need money now. I have registered at the **Stay Alive Clinic**. It's a **thousand naira** down payment and another thousand when the baby arrives.

'All right, we'll give you a thousand now. Cyn, dear, please get the money from the safe in my office.'

As soon as Cynthia left the room, Chinwe smiled at the Chief and made her usual intimate sign. She smiled encouragingly as he took a step towards her.

'Here you are, Uzo,' said Cynthia, who had quietly returned to the room and had witnessed the scene. 'My goodness!' she said to herself. 'That woman is really erotic. No wonder Uzo had found it difficult to break away. I wonder where all this will lead us?'

Chief Ubani had turned quickly on hearing her voice and he looked foolishly confused as well as embarrassed. He took the money from her, gave it to Chinwe who took it without a word of thanks and left the couple together.

This was the beginning of trouble, Cynthia thought later that night as she lay in her husband's arms and silently relived the scene with Chinwe in the office. Should she get involved? Her former resolve to stand by Uzo was melting fast.

She loved Nigeria but her real dream was to retire to their country house in **St Lucia** and shuttle between there and **Britain** where the children were. She would spend much time gardening, knitting for her grandchildren as they arrived, and generally idling away on the beach. It would be nice to have her husband with her as they grew old together, but with his acceptance of an 'outside' baby she no longer felt that they were one. She was no coward and it would be nice to defeat Chinwe and crush her totally, but would it be worth it at the end of the day?

Was not the intrusion of Chinwe the perfect excuse to call it quits with Uzo and go back to her roots and pass the rest of her days peacefully? His carelessness in not making sure that a girl could not claim she was carrying his baby hurt her. His not insisting that Chinwe had an abortion had hurt even more. Although he looked remorseful, did she not detect a tinge of smugness in him that he was apparently going to be a father again?

Cynthia tossed and turned all night trying to make a decision that would be fair to her family. Should she abandon Uzo to Chinwe?

'You have to weigh things very carefully,' cautioned Funmi the next day. 'Do nothing in haste.'

'What would you do in my place?' asked Cynthia.

'I would stay here with my husband,' said Funmi promptly. 'Your place is by Uzo. After so many mostly agreeable years together, why yield your place to a calculating devil? Whatever political heights he attains in future, you should be there to lend him your support.'

'What about all the humiliation from this affair?'

'Oh, come on, now, Cynthia,' said Funmi, laughing. 'What humiliation is there? What has taken place is no big deal anywhere in the world these days. Men will always have mistresses. What about the Greek Prime Minister who divorced his wife of 39 years some time ago, so he could marry his mistress who was in her twenties? That was a head of state, you know.'

'Yes, but the wife did not stay around to put up with the humiliation—she moved straight away to **America** while the old man was jetting around the world with the girl. I feel like doing the same.'

'You're not in that situation at all,' said Funmi. 'Uzo wants you. He doesn't want Chinwe or her child. It was all a dreadful mistake on his part but it is something a loving partner can forgive. Life's too short to dwell for long on a particular grievance.'

'That's precisely why I should pounce on this excuse to realise my own dream about what I really want for myself.'

'Which is?'

'To live out the rest of my life mainly in St Lucia; looking mainly after myself; playing the amiable granny from time to time; and generally doing my own thing. No heartache from a partner's possible infidelity.'

'That would mean no partner then, Cynthia.'

'Well...'

'You may not find peace and happiness that way.'

'I haven't tried it yet.'

'Anyway, I think you should remain here with Uzo.'

'I know I should, but Uzo's attitude may change once the baby arrives. He may want Chinwe for a wife, and she of course would want to have more kids for him. Where would I stand then?'

'Right where you are now, Cynthia,' Funmi told her emphatically. 'You're Uzo's lawfully wedded wife. Nothing can change that.'

'Divorce can, Funmi.'

'That's far-fetched in this matter—don't conjure it up.'

'Okay, I'm only being realistic, and that's why I feel I should use this opportunity to check out and avoid all the heartaches I know are lurking in the corner.'

'If you and Uzo plan things properly, you'll both have the last laugh on this matter. Chinwe's wicked machinations will all dissolve on her head and she'll lose out in the long run. Stay around and see it happen.'

Life went on normally in the Ubani household and soon campaigning for the senatorial elections began in earnest and Cynthia joined Uzo on the trail to canvas for votes in his constituency. It was hard work but she found it fun as she looked after him, making sure that he ate and slept well and was in top form. She was so engrossed in the activities that she forgot all about Chinwe.

That was until the day Uzo gave a party in the village square in his home town which formed a part of his constituency.

She was shocked to see Chinwe sitting with **Ifeoma** and **Ngozi**, two of Uzo's sisters. Her initial reaction was to seek out her husband in the male section and demand an explanation. She decided against that. Too immature. She also decided against going to ask her sisters-in-law what business Chinwe had there. No, that could lead to a telling-off from the ladies who had always resented their brother's closeness to her, and had done their best to make her feel like an outsider. Besides, Uzo must have introduced Chinwe to his extended family.

Cynthia decided to keep her cool—the party would soon be over. She served guests from **Enugu** and joined in the general gaiety. Uzo's speech was excellent and she went over later to hug him. Chinwe did not go near Uzo, but stuck to the sisters' company, carrying herself delicately, and when the crowd dispersed some hours later she disappeared into thin air. If Cynthia had not observed her throughout the party, she would have thought it had been a ghost she had seen.

As she bade her in-laws goodbye there was nothing in their behaviour which suggested that there had been something amiss. Ngozi and Ifeoma had been their usual indifferent selves.

On the way home Uzo looked so drained that she decided she would not disturb him with talk of Chinwe. However, Cynthia could not relax. She was fed up. She was impatient. She did not want a game of cat and mouse in which she would be waiting to see what Chinwe would do next. She wanted things to come to a head quickly so she could re-organise her life. She felt she was still young enough to enjoy life fully, and it did not necessarily have to involve a partner. She did not need this sort of upheaval at the onset of her retirement. Fate did mock people sometimes.

"Look, Uzo, you were right to accept this girl's pregnancy," said **Nneka**, his paternal aunt who was only a couple of years older than him. 'You must go one step further and make her your second wife.'

'Never!' exploded Chief Ubani. 'Never! I'm already riddled with guilt and remorse that I allowed her to claim she was expecting a baby for me. To have accepted the baby was sheer lunacy. I don't love or even like the girl, and what do I want with a baby, and that sort of baby? I forced my wife to stop at just two kids many years ago when she was younger than this Chinwe, and when the poor lady is now fifty, I go and accept a pregnancy from a girl. It's not fair at all and it isn't something that God will bless. I feel so bad.'

'What's there to feel bad about?' asked the aunt. 'You're a man and a chief. You're entitled to as many wives and children as you like, no matter the sort of marriage you have contracted. You're not poor. Having just two kids does not befit your image as a man of substance. Besides, these kids of yours do not reside in this country. They had only their primary and secondary education here. They really don't belong to this community.'

'They do, Nneka, they do. Don't forget that

they speak fluent **Igbo**, and have interacted very well here. They are not strangers at all. My daughter is married to a Nigerian, remember?'

'Yes, but he's a stranger too. He's from **Rivers State** and has lived most of his life abroad, and has taken your daughter to do the same. Your son may marry a foreign wife. Then where would you stand?'

'Stand where?'

'Amongst the sons of this soil. You would have no heir who belongs here. Look, Chinwe's presence in your life is a blessing. It was ordained by God. Now you will have a son and possibly several sons who will belong here. Then, an Igbo wife will be an asset to your political ambitions.'

'But I don't want her and I don't like polygamy,' protested Chief Ubani. 'My father has had only one wife all his life.'

'His is a different case. He's my brother, so I know. He could not afford to take another wife, and besides, your mother, **Mama**, had about twelve children even though only seven lived. I think this is an opportunity for you to have an indigenous wife and fit into the Igbo community. Tongues will now stop wagging about Cynthia wearing the trousers in your home.'

'If that's what people think, I can't be bothered. I love Cynthia and I want her with me always.'

'Hm, well, no one has said that you should do away with her. She certainly has her uses. I'm sure she must have—although these have always been lost on me. However, you don't seem unhappy with her, so that's all right. Chinwe can come and live with us in the village in the lovely house you have there, if you don't want her in your house in Enugu.'

'I can't have her with me. Never!'

'Don't be so vehement in your rejection of her. She could carry out her threats to destroy your political ambitions. These young ladies have no scruples.'

'And you want me to marry such a person, Nneka! I don't want her in my life.'

'Well, you'll have to tolerate her, at least for a while. We want you to win that senatorial seat and add to the numerous honours you have already brought to the family. We're all right behind you. Don't spoil it all by rejecting this girl for fear of what Cynthia will feel or do, and allowing her to make your opponents triumph over you. Think carefully, Uzo.'

'I don't want this girl.'

'We all know you don't, and we never would have known anything about her if she had not had the sense to come with her people and introduce herself to us. I can't understand why you don't like her. She's so mild-mannered and humble. I can't really believe that she issued threats if you rejected her.'

'She's a damn good actress.'

'Well, I suppose any woman would take any drastic step to see that her pregnancy is accepted by her lover. It takes two to tango.'

'I didn't reject the pregnancy.'

'No, but you rejected the girl. That's not fair to a would-be mother of your child, or even children.'

Chief Ubani left off arguing with his aunt, but before they parted she made him promise to tell Cynthia that, to stop Chinwe destroying his political ambitions, he would have to take her as a second wife.

Cynthia took the news sadly and calmly. She had been expecting such a thing since Chinwe's presence in the village.

'One thing is sure, Cyn,' said Chief Ubani, looking desperately unhappy, 'she can't come and live here with us. That can never happen.'

'But don't you think that's what she desperately wants? To live here with you as your only wife.'

'How can you say such a thing, Cyn? Live here? A place you and I worked hard to put together? Don't forget you're the co-owner of this place. There's no room for Chinwe here. None.'

Cynthia smiled sadly. Poor man! He looked so distraught. She wondered why it had not been the extended family which broke the news of a second wife to her. Maybe because she was a foreigner.

Usually the family did the dirty job for the man. The wife is summoned to a family gathering and the husband's new or hidden wife is introduced to her. Sometimes it is along with the child or children the mistress has had for the man. The wife is then asked to accept and welcome the lady and her kids as the family had obviously done. Some wives who had had no inkling of what had been going on were reported to have collapsed at these gatherings, and a few became psychiatric cases.

Cynthia was mature and experienced enough to know that marriage breakdown is not confined to any one ethnic group or country or race. If she had married Barry there was no guarantee that they would have still been together or that she would have been as happy with him as she had been with her husband.

However, with the news of a second wife, must she still stick it out in Nigeria? No.

Chief Ubani was shocked when she quietly told him that she could not share him with another woman whether in the same house or elsewhere. She had always found it ridiculous when at public functions, some men turn up with wives on either side of them. Or turning up at functions with a variety of wives, as the women take their turns at the various outings. She did not want such a thing in her life.

'I know the situation has been forced on you, Uzo, dear, but I can't accept it,' she told him.

'You want to destroy our home, Cyn?' he asked in a desperate voice.

'I'm destroying nothing. You are dismantling our union, Uzo. However, you need all the peace of mind you can get and that's why I'm hereby giving you the opportunity to have it. I'm not deserting you, but I need my peace of mind too. So I'll go and stay in London for a week and then go on to St Lucia. I'll live in London for a while when **Nkem's** baby arrives and after that things will sort themselves out.'

'What about me? How can you cold-heartedly toss me aside like that?'

Cynthia moved away from their bedroom that night and, three weeks later, she left for Britain.

'Hm, that's a pity,' Chief Ubani's aunt told him at the news of Cynthia's departure. 'That's a foreign wife for you. Our women would not throw such a good husband as you aside because of foolish pride. They would cooperate with you. What's wrong with having a mate? Anyway, perhaps her exit is for the best. Chinwe should move in with you right away. You need someone—a woman—to look after you.'

'I don't want Chinwe living with me,' protested Chief Ubani, feebly. The shock of his wife's departure had not left him, and afterwards it took very little persuasion from his sisters and his aunt to allow Chinwe to move in. He had, however, bluntly refused to go and meet her people and his female relations had done it for him.

Chinwe's parents had felt humiliated that he had not deemed it fit to come and meet them before sending his people, but they understood the situation well and were relieved that there would be no unmarried mother on their hands. The Chief, through his people, had said that all he was doing was to give shelter to the woman carrying his baby and that marriage would come later if it suited both of them.

CHAPTER 7

Chinwe's promotion from the poor side of the housing estate to the rich side was the talk of the area for some weeks, particularly among the womenfolk.

Her family was openly condemned for helping her break up the Ubani home and thereby depriving the estate of the very helpful services **Mrs Ubani** had given freely to those who needed them.

'Hm, I know many young women cannot get husbands these days but it is a very wicked sin to go and snatch a neighbour's husband,' Mrs Okpara commented loudly to another neighbour in the same block of flats as Chinwe's mother was passing by.

'Ah, my sister, I've never seen such greed,' said Mrs Madu, equally loudly. 'The poor madam had to scurry back to her country, leaving behind the luxurious house she had helped to build. She worked so hard to save up for that house.'

'Hm, you're telling me. Then a nonentity of a girl comes from nowhere and pushes Madam out with her pregnancy. Tell me, how can God ever bless such a union?'

'We shall see. She and her family will come to a nasty end. God is not asleep. He will deal with them all when He feels it's time to do so. We shall all be here to see them.'

Instead of going to look for her own husband she had to go and lure away another woman's.'

'Oh yes, and a rich and prominent man at that. I have three unmarried daughters, and I'm anxious to see them get married, but I'll never allow any of them to do such a thing. It's wicked and the end is bad.'

'Ha, some families have no shame. Ha!

The **Dozies** went about stealthily with disgrace stamped all over them and they did their best to avoid their neighbours.

'If this weren't our own place I would

suggest we move away,' said one of the sons.

'We can't,' said **Mrs Dozie**. 'We have nowhere else to go.'

'We could go back to the village.'

'And stay in that dilapidated family house? Never!' thundered **Mr Dozie**. 'We shall sit it out here. Chinwe has brought all this on us because of her unbridled greed and ambition. I don't really blame our neighbours for their criticisms. If only she had done the noble thing and had an abortion!'

'She should never have run after the man in the first place,' said **Dele**.

When Chinwe moved into Chief Ubani's house, he was away on one of his political campaigns. His aunt, Nneka, and his two sisters, Ifeoma and Ngozi, were at hand to receive her.

When she asked **Innocent** the steward for the key to the master bedroom, she was given a key to one of the guest rooms and

told that that had been the master's
instructions.

Chinwe felt hurt, but she moved in meekly.
Her in-laws stayed on to give the traditional
welcome to the new 'wife'.

When Chief Ubani returned five days later
he was in high spirits. His tour had been
successful and he was sure of winning the
senatorial seat in his constituency.

He was not pleased to see Chinwe installed
in his home, but he allowed himself to be
cajoled into bidding her welcome by his
aunt and sisters, and even organised a small
party for the purpose.

Chinwe glowed with pride and self-
fulfilment as she stood by his side receiving
the few guests who had turned up. She had
invited her people but no one came. That did
not disturb her happy state of mind.
Nwankego turned up glittering and bubbly,
and Chinwe proudly introduced her to Chief
Ubani. Nwankego moved easily among the
high-powered guests chatting familiarly.
Chinwe suspected some of them must have

been her boyfriends in the past.

I must not let her come too close now that I'm almost married to the Chief, Chinwe cautioned herself. *I'll never invite her here again.*

It was not an easy evening for her as she was openly snubbed by the few married ladies there, and the Chief did not make any effort to show that he cared for her. To a casual stranger, she could easily have been one of the guests, and an unimportant one at that.

When the last guest left, Chinwe quickly went to her room and changed into what she considered a sexy nightgown. She did not look too bad in spite of her bulge. After waiting in vain for the Chief to come to her, as he had done since he returned home, she went and knocked timidly on his door.

There was no response.

She opened the door and found him dressed for bed, but sitting at his desk poring over some letters. He looked up when she came into the room and nodded at her. Soon he put away his papers and sat down on the settee. She sat near him, smiled seductively and tried to look alluring. Chief Ubani appeared not to notice. She pouted and squirmed until he asked her if something was the matter.

'You're not feeling unwell, Chinwe, are you?' he asked anxiously.

'No, Chief, I thought I should come and bid you goodnight when you failed to come to my room.'

'Oh, I had things to do. I think I'll just go to sleep now. I have a full day tomorrow. Goodnight.'

'Goodnight, Chief,' she replied, waiting for him to give her a kiss or show some sign of affection. He merely smiled vaguely at her and headed for the bathroom, calling out to her to shut the bedroom door as she left. Chinwe felt very angry and disappointed that her control over Chief Ubani's passion was slipping.

The old shrivelled fool, she fumed to herself later in her room. *But for his money and position, I wouldn't go near him. Such a lousy lover. He has absolutely nothing to offer a girl like me. I should have left him to his cold wife. They deserve each other. Heaven knows what he will be like in a few years' time. He probably won't be able to do anything. He will definitely be past it. Anyway, that won't be a problem. I will have found someone else by then. Meanwhile, I'll enjoy his money and everything else which goes with a relationship with someone in his position.*

Thus comforted, Chinwe went to sleep.

The closeness she had envisaged between her and Chief Ubani did not materialise and he hardly even had any time for her. She put this down to his rigorous tours and her ungainly shape. He would be eating out of her hands once she produced his son and heir.

Of course her son would be his sole heir. His people would fully support her. After all, she was Igbo like them—unlike the West Indian wife. Her children for him would be full Igbos.

When her condition permitted, she accompanied him on some of his tours and did her best to get on with the party members and their wives, most of whom were Igbos. He seemed pleased when he noticed the efforts she was making to look after him during these trips.

The major discomfort she had was the attitude of the Chief's parents. They were neither loving nor hostile to her. They were polite but indifferent about her presence in their son's life. When she asked the Chief if they did not want her in the family he told her that they were old and anyway, at his age parents would not want to get too involved in his personal life.

She was not really unhappy in her new home and she did her best to improve the atmosphere around her by being more tolerant with the domestic workers. However, she loathed the way her in-laws popped in and out of the house as they liked and carted things away without asking her. Cynthia had taken away all the valuable household goods except the furniture, but

the Chief had replaced the essential ones.
These she considered hers as she was the
new mistress of the house.

One of the Chief's sisters 'borrowed' her
blender, another her yam-pounder, a
nephew, the portable television. There had
been angry silences whenever she had asked
for these items back, and no one ever did as
she asked.

'Are they doing this because I'm an Igbo?'
She had to ask the Chief one day. 'These are
people of my own age group; surely they
know they should not think along the old
line that everything in the house belongs to
the man and that his relatives have the right
to help themselves to whatever they like?'

The Chief looked at her curiously and
laughed, 'You're a cute little fighter, aren't
you? I knew that that meek front would
soon collapse and your true self would
emerge.'

Chinwe laughed too. 'You mean I pretend to
be submissive whereas I'm really not?'

'Er, yes. Well, that's not a fault. You're

merely trying to make things easy for yourself. Scheming is an essential part of human life.'

'Everyone's?'

'I think so. Tell me, Chinwe, why were you so keen to make my acquaintance?'

Chinwe looked at him, startled. She knew she could not stick to her story of wanting help for her widowed aunt. She could not tell him the real truth either.

'I was very much in love with you, Chief,' she lied, looking away from him.

Her declaration did not come as a surprise but he did not believe her. Women fell over themselves to get to know him, but none had gone the length Chinwe had gone— bribing his driver to make a stop so she could talk to him. The driver had confessed to the Chief the role he had played and he had warned the Chief to be careful in case Chinwe had been sent to kill or poison him. He had thanked the man with a handsome sum of money and then he had sacked him.

He studied Chinwe closely; discovered that all she wanted was a sugar-daddy to keep her in comfort, and then he relaxed. She was no different from most women who, as soon as they knew of a prominent or well-to-do man, immediately embarked on a scheme to offer their bodies to him for money. He had expected that sooner or later she would have got what she wanted and would then move on or wait to be dropped. News of her pregnancy, however, greatly puzzled him. Still, he did not believe that she had fallen in love with him, and jokes from his friends that a young woman rejuvenated an old man's blood failed to convince him that she should be in his house. But did he have a choice? The whole incident was badly timed. If it had happened at any other time of his life when he was not anxious to present a flawless image, he would have laughed at the little schemer and sent her packing.

Well, now he would have to treat her nicely even though he missed his wife badly. He missed the mature way Cynthia had run his home, leaving him in peace to face other things. It had been nice then, but looking back he felt Cynthia should not have worked hard to prove herself capable of coping. She should not have shouldered all the problems which cropped up. She should have involved him, or protested, no matter how much he complained and got him to help her. Then he would not have had the time and the peace of mind to go on an endless quest after other women.

With Chinwe, at first he enjoyed having a woman who did not have the answer to all the problems in the home. A woman who, in spite of his hectic schedule, still asked him to solve domestic problems. He felt involved and useful, even if it only involved employing a new house help or changing the curtains.

Soon, however, this feeling began to wear off as he found himself involved over minor issues. Chinwe was not to be put off.

'Here, Chief, How do you feel about your son moving in here?,' she once told him, taking his hand.

'Oh, no,' he exclaimed, pulling his hand away. 'I'm no good at such things. They make me feel funny. In fact, the sight of babies frightens me and I avoid them whenever I can. When they become human beings, say at the age of two or so, then I can tolerate them.'

Chinwe was taken aback by his comment and she wondered who would love the child. She knew she would do her best to make it feel wanted, but it would be difficult to be devoted to it. She did not have that sort of feeling in her; so if the father refused to adore it, well, Heaven help it. Anyway, she was in the Chief's place to enrich herself for the future; she must concentrate on that.

CHAPTER 8

'Oh no, you're wrong. It can't be a baby girl,' protested Chinwe vehemently when the midwife at the private hospital announced the baby's sex as soon as it arrived. 'It's a boy. It has to be. You're lying.'

'Ah, see my trouble,' said the midwife to her colleague who was trying to make Chinwe comfortable on the bed. 'Madam, please look properly now. This is the baby I've just got out of you. Here, look at the features carefully before I take her away.'

'Let's call in the senior nursing officer,' whispered the other nurse when Chinwe continued her protests.

The senior nursing officer came in and she tried to soothe Chinwe, telling her how beautiful the baby looked. When this failed to calm Chinwe down she gave instructions that the baby should not be taken out of the room until the director of the hospital had been sent for.

This was duly done and the hysterical mother was soothed until she fell asleep.

The Chief was away when the baby arrived but his aunt and his sisters rallied round mother and child when they arrived home and they were well taken care of.

Chinwe tried to feel happy. She had reconciled herself to the sex of the child and had even scolded herself for being so determined about having a baby boy. What did it matter, after all was said and done? A girl could be made heir of the father's property. All it required was a great effort on the part of the woman to make things work her way. Thank goodness that Cynthia had moved out—hopefully for good. What a relief it was to be relieved of the pregnancy! She quickly began to exercise so she could get back her figure.

Chief Ubani congratulated her warmly on his return but merely peeped into the cot at the baby.

His aunt was disappointed that, in spite of
her endless, 'She has your hair; she has your
eyebrows; she has your mouth,' he refused
to be enthusiastic about the baby.

It was as if they were trying to sell it to him.
This angered Chinwe and she had to tell her
in-laws that her mother would be moving in
to help look after the baby for a while.

They felt outraged at her decision but they
had to leave when Mrs Dozie moved in, and
two girls were employed to help out.

Chinwe's mother felt so ill-at-ease in the
Chief's house that she only stayed for one
week.

'Are you disappointed that it's a girl?'
Chinwe asked Chief Ubani.

'Oh no, I'm too broadminded for that sort of
attitude,' he said. 'The child is welcome.'

'Why did you ask my father to give it a
name?' Chinwe asked nervously. 'That was
most unusual. The name, at least the main
one, should come from you or your people.'

'Tradition, tradition,' he said, laughing. 'What's in a name?'

'Well, I hope you like the one my father gave: **Isioma**.'

'Isioma is fine.'

'So that's it, children,' said Cynthia to her children in London one evening. 'My going back to Enugu depends on your Dad. I've not abandoned him. I had to leave in order to allow him to see his way clearly to sort things out. He'll be all right. Meanwhile I'll go for a well-earned rest in St Lucia.'

Her widowed mother, who had returned home to St Lucia to live, was very glad to see her again, but was saddened by the news that her marriage was tottering.

'I hope it won't collapse totally,' she said.

'If it does, Mum, it won't be the end of the world,' said Cynthia.

'It won't be, but Uzo is such a nice and responsible person. I felt so proud having him as a son-in-law. Your Dad, too, was proud of him. He used to say that if he and

Uzo had been childhood friends, he would have risen to great academic heights too. Have you seen Barry?'

'Not yet, Mum. How's he doing?'

'He's doing fine. He has only himself and his son to look after.'

'Does he still have to look after his twenty-six-year-old son? The boy should be on his own now.'

'Maybe he is. They run the restaurant together.'

'I'll go see them later.'

Barry had retained his carefree look and attitude but was looking weather-beaten.

Cynthia's heart fluttered when they hugged and all the tender moments of their youth came rushing back. From hugging they went into a long kiss.

'I still feel something here for you, Cynthia,' he told her, laying a hand on his heart.

'I'd have been disappointed if you didn't,'

she laughed. 'In fact, I would have dropped dead at the discovery.'

'I'm serious, you know.'

'Are you now? You may be a widower, but I'm still married.'

'Sure you are. Now tell me everything. What went wrong over there in Nigeria?'

'Nothing. Everything's fine.'

'No, it isn't. Bad news has a way of getting around. People listen in at the telephone exchange. Ours is a small island, you know. Your marriage is on the rocks, isn't it?'

Cynthia had to admit that things had become a bit uncomfortable for her and she had had to get away for a while.

'Things have a way of sorting themselves out so sit back and relax. Luckily you have this lovely house by the sea and you've got your Mum and other relations to give you emotional support. Me, too, if you'll let me.'

'Thank you, Barry, dear, you're such a comfort.'

To ease the boredom of having nothing specific to do she began to help out at Barry's restaurant, mostly in the evenings. Business was slow and there was not much to do, but it was some distraction.

Because of the upheaval in her marriage she could hardly carry out any of the plans she had for a relaxed retirement, and could only manage the occasional gardening. It was hard not to indulge in self-pity and a feeling of injustice. What's more, she missed her husband. Yet she knew that if she had remained in that atmosphere in **Enugu**, trying to be heroic, she would soon have become a psychiatric case. She was lucky that, thanks to **Uzo**, money was not going to be a problem. There was no mortgage to be paid anywhere; rather, there was rent to be collected and the foreign bank accounts were in her name.

'Uzo is so nice and unselfish,' she told her mother one day when they were discussing the plight of women who get thrown out by their husbands without a dime to call their own. 'Imagine letting me be sole signatory to our bank accounts in **London**. Very few men in the **Western world** would allow such a thing, let alone in a society where everything in a home is considered the man's. I would marry Uzo all over again, but as a man in a different setting, not as a **Nigerian**. He encountered enormous hostility in his bid to make sure that cultural demands did not snuff the joy out of my life with him.'

'I'm glad you realise his worth,' said her mother.

'I do indeed, Mum, and that's why I still love him.'

'When will you go back there then?'

Cynthia did not answer.

Soon, she and Barry began a romantic relationship. This came as a surprise to no one. She saw it as a mature and convenient relationship and she toyed with the idea of remaining in it forever and never going back to Uzo. Where was the point in going back? He had survived ten months without her and was saddled with **Chinwe** and the baby girl. He did not need her any more. Their monthly telephone calls to each other had dwindled. As time went on they had less and less to talk about that would be considered 'safe'. He told her he was worried about the elections for, although he seemed more popular in his constituency than his opponent, he was not sure which way the votes would swing. People were so unreliable. She tried to soothe him, telling him to brace himself for whatever the outcome would be.

Frankly, she did not particularly care. She had become so happy with Barry, and felt so free and peaceful. The emotional insecurity associated with growing old was very much reduced since the tension of struggling to have a partner's full attention was no longer there.

She did not mind the menopause; she did not mind Barry eyeing younger women; she did not mind whatever Uzo did with himself in Enugu. She did not feel committed to any man and therefore her pride was not at stake.

This evident emotional independence displeased Barry and he began to press her to live with him or let him live with her. She told him that was a crazy request to make, and her mother agreed with her. Their relationship cooled off for a while, and then it took off again on her return from seeing her new grandchild in London.

She had to stop going over to help out at the restaurant when he kept sacking his cooks, thereby forcing her into a situation where she had to offer her services in the kitchen.

She saw this as a ploy to obtain free labour on his part. He looked hurt as he denied the accusation and he told her to stop coming over if that was how she felt.

She stopped going there but their relationship continued. Cynthia was not happy with the situation.

'Prophet John,' said Chinwe, 'I'm not happy with the way things are.'

'Why not?'

'Our prayers don't seem to produce the

desired results. You said I would have a baby boy, but I had a baby girl. You said the Chief would cut off all contact with his wife, but he hasn't. He telephones her regularly and consults with her even on minor issues. As for our baby, he doesn't know she even exists.'

'Except the Lord builds the house, he labours in vain who builds it,' intoned **Prophet John** in response. Except the Lord keeps watch over the city, the watchman keepeth awake in vain. You have to allow the Lord to do His will.'

'If that's your view, why did you ask me for large sums of money so you could offer special prayers and perform some ceremonies which would ensure that what I wanted came through?'

'It is good to present your request before God.'

'Yes, but you assured me that...'

'You have to pray with optimism and a lot of faith. Faith can move mountains.'

'But it didn't bring me a baby boy or bind my husband to me. In fact, I think he very much loathes my presence in his house. Your prayers can't be effective.'

'They got you pregnant.'

'Yes, but...'

'So, praise the Lord! If you want the Chief to love no one else but you there are certain things I could do for you. The process is expensive.'

'Not again! We've done that several times.'

'Once, I think and it did get you the Chief and send out the wife; so my prayers are quite effective. If you didn't get all your desired results, then that's the way God wants it. I'm not God, so don't blame me for anything. No one has ever complained about my work. You can stop coming here if you have no faith in my work.'

'Oh, don't be angry, Prophet John,' pleaded Chinwe. 'Here's some money. Do something so that the Chief will love me and my child and will make provision of a house for us.

He's getting old, and with the rate people drop dead these days, I could be a widow at any time. I don't pray for that but I have to be realistic and think of the future.'

'That's true. I'll do my best, but remember, unless the Lord...'

'Yes, yes, yes,' said Chinwe, getting up hastily. 'Do your best, please.'

Chinwe used all the concoctions she had been given by Prophet John to draw the Chief to her and she waited to get him in a good mood so she could make her request. The snag was that he was hardly ever in a good mood. They did not quarrel and she was comfortable, but she did not feel a part of him. He treated her with calculated politeness, as if she and her child were his guests. He had stopped making love to her.

Well, that had not bothered her much. She was living with him now and many people considered them married. The future looked rosy, for soon she would become a senator's 'wife'. How people would envy her!

She soon got impatient, however, waiting to

talk to Chief Ubani about making property available for her child, and she decided to find out how the land lay.

Unknown to him she had found the combination to his safe and she knew where he kept the spare key to his room.

So, when he was away on one of his trips, she let herself into his room, opened the safe and settled down to going through his private files. As she read the documents, she went numb and faint. Then anger took over. 'Why, the bastard has nothing—absolutely nothing of his own!' she exclaimed to herself. 'The house here is in the name of his two kids; of the two houses in London, one is in Cynthia's name, and the other in their kids' names. The one in **St Lucia** belongs to her. Only the one in his village belongs to him, and that's nothing to shout about. So he was truly under that woman's wrap as rumours had it! What *juju* did she use on him? Ha! Ha! Ha!' She began to laugh in a demented way. 'What a farce! So Cynthia's kids can come and eject me from this place at any time! All my planning and plotting has been in vain! I wouldn't be surprised to find they run a joint account. Yes, they do!'

The next drawer confirmed that. Cynthia had signed a booklet of blank cheques before she left.

At that point, Chinwe fell down senseless. When she came to, she was in bed in her room. Her mother was in a chair nearby. She could hear the Chief's voice in the sitting room talking to some visitors. She panicked and sat up.

'The Chief's back?' she asked her mother, trying to keep the panic out of her voice. Her mother nodded silently.

'Who brought me here?'

'I don't know. I think he asked the domestic help when he found you lifeless in his room, with his safe open and his documents scattered all over the place.'

'Did he ask you to come and take me home?'

'He didn't say that. He merely said I should come and stay with you until his aunt and sisters arrive tonight. He's sent for them.'

'Sent for them! What for? Those domineering women! I won't have them here. He knows how I feel about them. I'm the mistress in this house now; he'll have to listen to me.'

'Pipe down, Chinwe, and be careful,' cautioned **Mrs Dozie**. 'That was a serious offence you committed.'

'What serious offence?' shouted Chinwe. 'Going through my husband's documents is not a criminal offence, or an offence of any sort. We are one. He's entitled to go through my things if he wishes. He knows that.'

'Well, I'm not learned,' said Mrs Dozie, 'but even if you were lawfully married to him, you'd have to tread softly. Don't provoke him into ending the relationship. He could abandon you and the baby and you'll both suffer.'

'He can't do that. One word from me to the outside world about such a thing and his political ambition would be ruined. He's not a fool. He won't send me away. He dare not.'

'Hm, if you had listened to me you wouldn't have found yourself in this unholy set-up. Anyone who deliberately ousts a woman from her matrimonial home faces the wrath of God. Justice may be delayed but it will surely come. The whole thing frightens me. The one who will suffer the most is poor **Isioma**.'

'She won't suffer. The Chief is responsible enough to provide for his child. She may not inherit a house from him, but she will be all right for life.'

Mrs Dozie had to keep silent in the face of such optimism.

When the visitors left, Chinwe got up, saying she was quite fit. She persuaded her mother to leave.

'Do you feel all right, Chinwe?' asked the Chief, looking quite concerned when she went into the sitting room.

His attitude surprised her for she had come prepared to face his wrath. She went down on her knees and asked for his forgiveness. Pulling her up to her feet, he hugged her, telling her that it was natural for her to be curious about his affairs. However, it would have been tidier if she had asked to be told whatever she needed to know, rather than breaking into his room.

That night he came to her room. His sisters did not come. Chinwe relaxed. The Prophet's prayers must be working. There was still hope.

CHAPTER 9

Chief Ubani let out a long hiss of disgust when the results of the senatorial seat in his constituency were announced on radio. He and a close party friend, **Chief Amadi**, were at his hotel suite hideout. He had been so sure of victory that for a minute the news did not actually sink in. '**Chief Chuka Obosi** scored 13,251 votes: Chief Uzoamaka Ubani scored 10,813 votes,' the newscaster had announced.

'You mean I've lost to an idiot like Obosi?' he exploded with unrestrained fury. 'I know he's a lawyer like myself and there isn't really much difference between our two parties, but this is a question of personality. What positive contribution can a man like him make at the Senate?'

'I don't know,' said Chief Amadi. 'The man can hardly express himself clearly in any known language and his reasoning is like a child's. That was why he opted out of the law practice to go into business. I'm sure these results will surprise everybody. You were the popular choice.'

'So I thought too. After all, it was my people who sent a delegation to me urging me to go into politics. Cynthia warned me not to, but I thought I would be able to make some valuable contributions. I spent a lot of my time, money and effort on campaigns.

I even neglected my practice and thereby lost huge sums of money only to suffer defeat at the hands of a totally unworthy man.'

'I know, I know. Well, take it like a man. Obosi spent a lot of money bribing people with money and foodstuffs so they would vote for him.'

'He'll only bring disgrace to them. Anyway, that's not my headache. I've had my belly full of politics.'

'Oh no, Uzo, you're not a coward. You shouldn't give up that easily. You're one of our finest sons.'

'I don't believe that.'

'That's no flattery. You'll have to try again. Four years will soon come and go. You'll get in easily then. No one will re-elect that buffoon.'

'Thanks for your loyalty, but I'm through, really through with politics. I'm not cut out for it here. Cynthia, who told me that she gave me her support, may be disappointed with the results, but she'll be greatly relieved.'

'How is she?'

'Fine. She's in St Lucia at the moment. I'll join her there for a long holiday after seeing my grandchild in London. I need to get away from here for a while.'

Cynthia took the news of the defeat quietly when Uzo phoned. She told him it was probably for the best since she had never believed that the country was ready yet for his brand of politics.

He told her all that was behind him and that he would be joining her shortly and then they would both return to Enugu.

She was silent.

'Cyn, are you there?' he asked anxiously.

'Yes, dear, I'm here.'

'Did you hear me? I said after my holiday, we'll both come back here and resume our lives quietly. I promise you I won't dabble into politics again. Ever!'

'Good, but I don't think I want to come back to Enugu,' she told him. 'I'm happy where I am, here.'

'What? Did I hear you right, Cyn? Did you say you don't want to return home?'

'Yes, Uzo.'

'Why?'

'You've got someone with you there. You can't have both of us.'

'There's never been a question of having both of you. You and I planned that, win or lose, you'll return home and we'll both continue our lives together.'

'Yes, I know, but...'

'Is it because of Barry? Are you leaving me for Barry? He doesn't love you and he doesn't need you. Besides, he has a record of his wives dying on him. You don't want to be next on his list, do you? Seriously speaking, I both love and need you. Our children, too. Cyn, don't you still love me?'

'Of course I do, Uzo, and Barry's only a caring friend like he's always been.'

'Good. Now, get prepared to return to your lawful place which is right here by me, wherever I happen to be.'

'What about that woman?'

'That woman returns to wherever she came from. That was our plan, remember, Cyn? Your plan, actually. At the time, I was all for coming out plain and damning the consequences, but you said it was best to cooperate, allow her in so as not to ruin my chances of being elected and then later, send her away. I reluctantly agreed with you and then you left and I allowed her in. But for your suggestion, she and whatever burden she was carrying would have been long forgotten now. You've imposed her on me for too long and I can't take it any longer. I don't want her.'

'All right, all right, Uzo. I know it was my idea that she should be allowed to move in until after the elections, to quieten things down, but hasn't something developed between you? She's Nigerian and I'm not. Isn't she more useful to you all round?'

'Stop talking rubbish, Cyn. Is Barry there with you? Let me speak to him. He must not ruin my home.'

'Why should Barry be with me, and what's all this talk about him, anyway?'

'Okay, maybe he's not terribly important to you. So what it means is that you saw Chinwe's case as an opportunity to break away from me and live on your own. It's probably a scheme you've had up your sleeve all the time. Chinwe was a convenient excuse, seeing the way you eagerly gave up your place to her. I thought you had our family's interest at heart, now

I'm not so sure. This is all so disappointing.'

'All right, Uzo, I'll return home with you when you come. Make sure you tidy up everything before you leave.'

Cynthia sat down by the telephone deep in thought afterwards. She loved Uzo and wanted to be with him, but she also cherished her independence. Maybe deep down she was tired of being a wife and having to be 'on duty' all the time.

Her no-strings-attached relationship with Barry was also enjoyable to a certain extent, but common sense told her that, as time went on, she would have to be 'on duty' in that relationship too.

Women with partners of any sort never really go into retirement. However, did she actually want to hand over her home permanently to that scheming Chinwe and her child?

Chinwe was highly delighted when the Chief told her that the driver would take her down to his village to spend some time with his people. He would join her there later that day.

She had no doubt in her mind that they were going to tell her that she had been accepted into the family, and that a delegation was going to be sent to meet her people to talk about marriage.

She felt so relieved, for even though she had a baby for Chief Ubani and was living with him, she could not really claim to be his wife even in the traditional way. If only he would go and meet her father formally and then send his people to him! This had been her secret desire since the baby had arrived and she had hoped that in the euphoria of winning in the elections he would comply with her wish and then she would be all right. She would be a force to be reckoned with in the family whether Cynthia returned or not.

Unfortunately he had lost in the elections and she did not dare bring up such an issue. She had been a bit apprehensive that he would take out his frustration on her since she was living closest to him, but he had been such a gentleman that even when she had appeared downcast that he had not won he had told her to cheer up, that it was not the end of the world. As for him, a few days after the results of the elections he had brightened up and resumed full-time work in his office. He seemed in high spirits and she began to think of ways by which she could keep him in that mood. She sang all the way to the Chief's village where she was received by his aunt and two younger sisters.

When she inquired after his parents, for whom she had brought some gifts, she was told that they had gone visiting relatives at a neighbouring village and would be back some days later.

Chinwe was surprised. She felt it was odd that her prospective parents-in-law should be away when she had been invited to spend some time with the family, but she kept her thoughts to herself.

Actually, they had never drawn her close to them, but merely treated her like a friend to their son. They had never touched Isioma or even referred to her in a conversation.

Well, that was their loss, Chinwe told herself. It was their son she lived with, not them.

After lunch Chinwe was called to a family meeting comprising two elderly men, five elderly women including aunt **Nneka**, the Chief's elder sisters, and some other members of his extended family.

Chief Madu was the spokesman.

'Yes, Miss Chinwe,' he said, 'we have called you to this gathering to tell you that your brief relationship with our son Chief Uzoamaka Ubani is over. You will return to your parents' house.'

Chinwe was confused. She could not believe her ears.

'Return to my parents' house, sir?' she asked. 'You can't make me do that. What offence have I committed? I wasn't responsible for the Chief's defeat. In fact I felt it very badly.'

'No one is accusing you of that. It has nothing to do with the purpose of this gathering,' said Chief Madu. 'The point is that our son has told us that he doesn't want you in his house, nor in his life, any longer. You will go back to your people. We are not asking for a refund of the money or gifts our female folk took to your family when you came to live with our son—we don't do that in this family. We just want you to leave and stay away from our son.'

'But you can't take a decision like that, my elders,' said Chinwe in a conciliatory voice. 'My husband should have—'

'Point of correction, Miss Chinwe,' said the other male relative. 'If by "my husband" you're referring to our son Chief Uzoamaka Ubani, then you're wrong. You're not married to him.'

'I think I am.'

'Did he ever propose to you?'

'No, but—'

'Has he formally met your father?'

'No, they've never really met, but—'

'So, according to our tradition he is not your husband. He never told us that he wanted you for a wife or that he wanted you to live with him. You were the one who ran to introduce yourself to us as the girl expecting a baby for him. We asked him about it, and while accepting that he made love to you he said you were not even a girlfriend and that he was not the father of the baby you were expecting.'

'Impossible!' exclaimed Chinwe, jumping to her feet. 'He's the father of my baby. This is the first time I've been told he isn't. He never told me that. He never rejected the pregnancy.'

'Did he accept it? Did his parents give it a name?'

'No.'

'Who gave the baby a name?'

'My father did.'

'Then the baby belongs to your family. I'm sure your parents know that.'

'But my father is entitled by tradition to

give a name to his grandchildren.'

'Yes, but not the main name for his daughter's child if the child is accepted by the supposed father. Children here belong to their father's family.'

'Anyway, my elders, I can't claim to know why the Chief did not want to give a name to our daughter, but she is his. Look, she looks very much like him. Everyone says so, even aunt Nneka here.'

'That is not our business,' snapped the elder aunt to the Chief. 'The baby doesn't belong to our son. He can't be the father.'

'He is! He is!' cried a near demented Chinwe. 'He made love to me and I became pregnant. He's the father of this baby, no matter what anyone says. The Chief is only finding an excuse to abandon me and the baby.'

'He doesn't want you in his life any longer, so that's that,' said **Ngozi**. 'He was never your husband. He merely took compassion on your state of homelessness, and you had to ruin it all by breaking into his safe. What a disgraceful thing for a university graduate to do.'

'So that's it? Let me tell you I have the right to go into my husband's room and go through his things. He told me so himself. He was not angry with me.'

'He wasn't because you meant nothing to him,' said Chief Madu. 'You were only a guest there. Anyway, this evening you will be returned to your parents' home. Our son has been very generous. He has provided **forty thousand naira** to help you since you have no job.'

'Forty thousand! That's nothing, and anyway I won't accept that alone. There should be a monthly maintenance allowance for the baby until she's completed her studies at the highest level she can reach and got a job. She's his responsibility. He knows that as a lawyer. Does he want to be taken to court for that?'

There was an uproar from members of the family at Chinwe's boldness. The younger women were prepared to beat her up, but were restrained by the older ones.

'Look, I'm fed up with all this,' said the Chief's aunt. 'Tell this tramp the truth about our brother. If you had told us the female folk much earlier we would not have committed the folly of getting her into our brother's house. Telling her the truth is the only way of getting her out of our hair forever.'

'Hm,' hissed **Ifeoma**, 'she thinks she's smart and can get away with giving us a baby who is not our brother's.'

The two elderly men conferred in low tones for a while and then Chief Madu cleared his throat.

He announced to Chinwe that, due to an accident Chief Ubani had had when he had come home on holiday from **Britain** many years ago, he developed an illness which rendered him **infertile** even though he was still quite virile. This was why his wife, who had wanted lots of children, could not have more than the two they had then. The matter was known only to a handful of the male elders of the family, and over the years there had been no question of extra wives and outside babies and no need to bring the issue to light. Chief Madu emphasised that there was nothing for the family to be ashamed about in the Chief's condition which had been confirmed both here and abroad, and that he still had regular tests to find out if the condition had been miraculously rectified. The Chief had been to a specialist immediately Chinwe told him she was expecting a baby for him. Sadly, the situation was still the same, so the baby could not be his. Records were at the **Teaching Hospital** to show the truth and the Chief was ready to submit himself to further tests and he would not mind the findings being made public. He would rather have this than continue to accept a child which was not his. He had been too polite to accuse Chinwe of sleeping around and then trying to pin another man's pregnancy on him; that was why he and Cynthia had made the offer they did.

'You should have accepted that offer,' said Ngozi, 'and you would have saved yourself

all the problems you're going to have from
now on.'

'Better still, you should have had an
abortion when he failed to approach your
people at the early stage,' remarked Ifeoma.

Chinwe looked dumbfounded and
shamefaced. Deep down she knew they had
told her the truth. Months of taking fertility
drugs had failed to make her pregnant for
the Chief and she had begun to wonder what
was wrong. She only became pregnant on
Ifeanyi's return from a three-month course
from abroad when they made love. She was
not sure then whose pregnancy she was
carrying, and her mind had told her that it
was Ifeanyi's, but since it was the Chief she
wanted, it had to be his. If he had protested
vehemently then she would have told
Ifeanyi it was his and he might have
married her. After all, he knew nothing of
her relationship with the Chief then.

She reflected on her relationship with Chief
Ubani which had lasted such a short time.
She felt a great sense of loss. Her flirtation
with wealth and power had been heady and

enjoyable, even though brief and sometimes fraught with humiliation.

She would have to make other plans to uplift herself.

She accepted the money Chief Ubani offered through Chief Madu, and signed the relevant documents without taking the trouble to go through them. If she had had the money she would have liked to drag the Chief through the courts to cause him some discomfort. She knew she would not win but she would have liked to see him suffer to a certain extent for all his scheming against her. How foolish she had been! She now understood that the Chief accepted the pregnancy merely to satisfy his own selfish ends at the time. Sooner or later, he would have chucked her and Isioma out of his life when it suited him and his wife. She felt great anger. To think that he had connived with the wife to leave and allow her to move in and have a false sense of security so she could be kept quiet for a while!

Ha! She had been lucky! The couple could have arranged for her to be murdered

secretly by hired assassins and then the
Chief would have declared her missing. No
one would have suspected anything since
there had been no dispute about the
pregnancy.

On her way home from the village she
thought of her condition. If only she did not
have Isioma to think of! She looked at her.
She did not feel loving and protective
towards her. In fact, with the development
of her paternity, she had become a burden.
She would have to be dumped with Mrs
Dozie. Chinwe wanted to remain a free soul
and live on the other side of town and try to
attract wealthy men.

Her parents took her return painfully and
silently. There were no recriminations. Mrs
Dozie agreed to look after Isioma while
Chinwe got a flat and looked for a job. She
could only stay for a few days before going
into hiding to escape the openly cruel
remarks from neighbours who felt she had
deserved what she got.

She sought refuge with **Nwankego** who took
pity on her. Together they planned Chinwe's

future. She took Nwankego's advice and bought a two-bedroom flat in a government housing estate outright from the owner for **N 30,000**. She was left with **ten thousand naira** from the money she was given by Chief Ubani.

'Now you have a base for life,' remarked Nwankego.

'That's true, but the nagging problem is that of Isioma's paternity. If I had only had cause to suspect that the Chief was infertile, I would have given her my surname as is the practice in a situation like mine. What do I do now? Her birth certificate bears his name.'

'What's in a name? You can change any part of your name at any time.'

'Shouldn't I give her Ifeanyi's surname?'

'Tell him first. Actually, she looks more like you and him than you and the Chief. I had not wanted to make that remark, but it's true.'

Ifeanyi shook his head sadly when Chinwe

finished her story.

'I'm sorry, Chinwe, but I can't accept the baby as mine,' he told her. 'We saw each other several times while you were pregnant and you never told me that you were carrying my baby. I'm not saying she could not be mine, but since you considered me too poor to be declared the father either openly or secretly, I don't feel obliged to consider her as mine.'

'Don't be angry, Ifeanyi,' pleaded Chinwe. 'I was merely obeying the Chief's orders. He kicked his wife out, like I said, so he could marry me. I was infatuated with him and I went along with the idea, but after our traditional wedding, I had to tell him the pregnancy wasn't his, but yours. He felt scandalised and he said that he would see to the end of your career if I made the truth openly known. I was afraid for your job, Ifeanyi. Maybe I have been foolish, but you know I do love you, don't you?'

'Why doesn't he want the baby now?'

'He does, but I'm refusing to give it to him because he has invited his wife back and they both want to raise **Isioma** in their home. You know how these foreign wives are about such things. I won't have that sort of thing at any price. I would become a stranger to my own child, a child who does not truly belong to that home.'

Ifeanyi shook his head again and told Chinwe firmly that he had no place whatsoever in the situation although he could see her point and sympathised with her. He did not want her ever to contact him on the issue again.

When he left, Chinwe broke down and flung herself on her bed in her sparsely furnished flat, weeping uncontrollably. She remained indoors for days, crying over the mess she had made of her life. She blamed everyone else but herself for her misfortune.

'Pull yourself together,' counselled Nwankego. 'It's not the end of the world if you don't have a father for your child. Even men who accept they are fathers shirk their responsibility. Look at me—I'm father and mother to my kids and they are none the worse off for it.'

'I know, but why should such a thing happen to me?' wailed Chinwe. 'I have to start all over again looking for a man who will support me financially.'

'Why look for a man to do that?' asked Nwankego in wonder.

'How else will I look after myself and Isioma comfortably? A man has to help.'

'Really? I can't believe it. Out there are millions of women, single or married, slugging it out at one job or another, to look after a string of kids. You have just one and you're moaning and waiting for a man to support you. That attitude is outdated when most women are striving for financial independence.'

'I know all that, Nwankego, but I'm used to being looked after by a man. With a fatherless baby, I won't be able to cope financially.'

'Is that so? Well, you'll have to retrain yourself. Get a job and make a home for yourself and Isioma. Any profitable romantic relationship would be welcome but you won't hang all your existence on that. Talking of Isioma, your mother sent someone over to say that the baby's slightly ill and might be pining for you. Didn't you tell your people you had moved from my place?'

'No, I don't want to be bothered.'

'I see. Well, I know how you feel, but don't abandon your child. Try and see her tonight.'

'I'll do that.'

Chinwe did not go to her parents' to see Isioma. Instead she went to Prophet John's church.

'My goodness, you've gone terribly thin!' he exclaimed on seeing her. 'Have you been ill?'

Chinwe poured out her woes.

'Do me a favour, please, Prophet John,' she pleaded.

'What is it?'

'Don't preach to me with your favourite quote.'

'Oh, you mean, "Unless the Lord builds the house he..."'

'Yes, I can't bear to hear it one more time. What I want now are strong prayers so I can find a man.'

Prophet John went pensive for a while, stroking his chin. When he came out of his trance, he advised her to sit up and take charge of her own life. She had not been using her God-given gifts to stand on her own feet; that was why things had not worked out well for her. God had given her good health, good education and a strong will and all she had done so far had been to use men as an access to a life of ease. This was wrong.

Chinwe hissed with impatience as she got up. 'You're entitled to your views on life,

Prophet John,' she said. 'I didn't come here to be preached to. If you're not capable of rendering me further services, I'll consult another prayerist. There's no shortage of effective ones.'

Prophet John shook his head sadly and shrugged. 'They'll only take your money for nothing. "Except the Lord builds the house, he labours in vain who..."'

Chinwe hurried out of the church. Throughout that night her thoughts were in turmoil. Money was running out and there was no one to turn to. Oh well, she would have a good sleep first and tackle the problem the next day.

There was a banging on the front door.

'Chinwe, Chinwe,' shouted a voice, cutting right into her dreams. 'Open the door! Are you all right?'

Chinwe woke up with a start and staggered over to open the door to **Dele**, one of her brothers.

'Sshh, don't shout. You'll wake up the whole neighbourhood,' she cautioned.

'It's almost two o'clock,' said Dele. 'People are at work. Chinwe, the most terrible thing has happened. We sent a message to you through Nwankego yesterday afternoon and waited all night for you to come.'

'Nwankego gave me your message, but I couldn't come. I was very troubled and I had to go to the church to pray.'

'To pray? Well, er, well, er, Isioma passed on this morning.'

'Passed on? What does that mean?'

'She died just before five this morning. She was restless the whole night. Mama was going to take her to the doctor in the morning, but... Oh dear, we all feel terrible. If only you had been there! We've been trying to get you since it happened, but couldn't since you had not given us your address. We had to go to Nwankego's office. Chinwe, I'm terribly sorry, but we all did our best for Isioma.'

Chinwe sat down in a chair, chin in hand, eyes staring vacantly into space. Dele put his arm about her.

'Chinwe, take heart. You'll be all right. You'll have other kids. God knows best. Try and put the past behind you. Get a job—that will be the best therapy. You'll survive. Release the tears, if you like. You'll feel better.'

'There are no tears to release,' said Chinwe slowly. 'I've shed all the tears I'm capable of shedding this past week. There are none left. Poor, poor Isioma. So she died! She didn't have much of a life, did she? What sort of life would she have had anyway, rejected as she was?'

'Don't talk like that, Chinwe,' admonished Dele in a shocked voice. 'We all loved her.'

'Hm, I've been selfish. I brought her into the world so I could use her to ensure a comfortable life for myself. I failed woefully and now she's gone. Poor, poor thing! I'm wicked. Yes, I'm wicked. Ha! Ha! Ha!'

'Stop, Chinwe, stop!' cried Dele in alarm. 'Don't lose your mind. Stop.'

'I won't lose my mind. I know precisely what I'm saying. "Except the Lord builds the house, he labours in vain who builds it." How very just!'

'What does that mean?'

'Ask Prophet John. He knows.'